About the author

Rishabh Puri is a highly accomplished entrepreneur of Indian origin with his spurring business set ups in Nigeria, Dubai, and China.

He was diagnosed with a life-threatening heart disease at the age of 1. His life was mostly limited to talking to the doctors and visiting hospitals for several major surgeries and regular check-ups, making him crave for a 'normal life'.

Reading and writing have always been a hobby for him. His maiden book, *Inside the Heart of Hope*, released in 2016 and was well appreciated by readers. His writings are mostly centered on hope, love, life; feelings that mankind needs in the recent times.

Rishabh is also an avid traveller, a supercar enthusiast, a Romantic chef over the weekend, a natural drawer, a hookah+green tea combination lover, and an active volunteer for supporting the needy.

Rishabh makes his home in Lagos, Nigeria and Dubai, UAE. He keeps coming back to India and stays in Chandigarh, his birthplace, which is so close to his faulty heart, for obvious reasons.

Seductive affair

RISHABH PURI

Srishti
PUBLISHERS & DISTRIBUTORS

Srishti Publishers & Distributors
Registered Office: N-16, C.R. Park
New Delhi – 110 019
Corporate Office: 212A, Peacock Lane
Shahpur Jat, New Delhi – 110 049
editorial@srishtipublishers.com

First published by
Srishti Publishers & Distributors in 2018

10 9 8 7 6 5 4 3 2

This is a work of fiction. The characters, places, organisations and events described in this book are either a work of the author's imagination or have been used fictitiously. Any resemblance to people, living or dead, places, events, communities or organisations is purely coincidental.

Printed and bound in India

Acknowledgements

Every day is a miracle. A chance for your fortunes to change, blessings to fall upon you like rain. Every day you might see a new mercy, sing a new song, or feel joy like you've never felt before. I am thankful that today, you've picked up my novel and have decided to read it.

Not every day of my life has been one blessed with health and good fortune. In fact, many of my days have been ones of suffering and loneliness. From my diagnosis with a rare disease, while I was still in infancy, to the surgeries I've had to undergo as a result, and the sleepless nights filled with gruelling pain I've had to suffer through, I have had some bad luck in my life.

But out of it has come the ability to write truths, a deeper appreciation for the life I live, and above all, an overwhelming gratitude for the people with whom I share this life. I'm blessed with the opportunity to thank them, and I'd like to take that opportunity now.

First and foremost, I'd like to thank God for the overwhelming blessings He has graced me with, and the joy I've felt in this life. I would also like to thank my mother, father, and sister for their love and support throughout my whole life. Not everyone is as graced as I am with a family that loves and cares for me the way they do. Without you, I would be lost.

I would like to thank my doctor, Alok Suryavanshi, who has stood by my side and taken incredible risks to give me a full, healthy life, and find for me a reprieve from the pain I feel. Doctor Dennis Lox, thank you for the countless hours you've devoted to my case and your expertise. Also, thank you for making me laugh on some of the darkest days of my life. Your care for me has strengthened me beyond belief. To Doctor Saminathan Suresh Nathan, my gratitude for the years of study and expertise that led me to you is beyond what words can communicate. Your work has changed my life for the better. I am beyond grateful.

And finally, I would like to thank you, dear reader, for opening this book. It is not every day that gives birth to a project of passion. It is not every day that a man can wake up to see one of his dreams realized for all to see and enjoy. What you are reading today is a product of my passion, one of my dreams brought to life. So today is an incredible day. Thank you for reading. I hope you enjoy.

Prologue

If you had told me what was coming, I would have never believed you. If someone had sat me down the very first day, before I even left the house, before I took the story, before I so much as laid my eyes on him, and told me what was going to happen, there wasn't a chance I would have believed them.

In retrospect, it was clear that my entire life had been leading to the moment before I stepped out of that door. One chapter of my life had come to an end, and another was just picking up. But, like all things in life, it simply didn't feel that much had changed. Yes, I had finished university – but I was still living with my mother, still at home, still sitting around most of the time while I tried to find myself a job that wasn't a complete dead end. I was doing what dozens and dozens of my friends were doing, hoping for the best and planning for the worst. And yet, without my knowing it, my life was about to change almost beyond recognition.

I took a deep breath and patted my hair into place the Nth time that morning. It looked fine – or at least it wasn't going to look any better – but I was still trying to find ways to avoid stepping out my front door and into my first day of work.

"You look fine," my mother's voice took me by surprise as she emerged from the kitchen to find me frowning at myself in the hallway mirror. "Come on, you're going to be late if you wait any longer."

"I know," I sighed, and reached for my bag. I hadn't spent a lot of money since I had graduated a few months back, but this had been one of my biggest splurges, a handbag that doubled for a briefcase. It made me feel professional and pulled-together, even though I felt like I was playing dress-up in someone else's clothes right then and there. Even with my long, usually unruly curly dark hair pulled back into a bun on top of my head and concealer carefully dotted beneath each of my eyes to hide the dark circles that had appeared from tossing and turning all night in nervousness, I still didn't feel right. I had had a long, lanky body all through my teen years and it was only in the last couple of months that I had actually developed anything resembling curves, and I was still getting used to the way clothes hugged me in places they hadn't before. Even though my breasts were still pretty small, the shirt strained over them in a way I wasn't certain I liked. I had tried this outfit on the night before and thought I looked good – cute, even, with my hair drawn up to show off my eyes which I had brought out with a slick of mascara. But today, I couldn't muster the same confidence.

"You look lovely," Mum reached over and patted down a strand of hair. "All the men in the office will be falling over you."

"I don't want that," I raised my eyebrows at her. "I'm not there to find a husband, remember?"

She pursed her lips at me, and I returned my gaze to the mirror, peering at myself critically. Okay, yes, I didn't look bad. The flecks of green in my otherwise dark brown eyes were practically glowing with excitement, and the heels added a couple of well-needed extra inches to my short frame. I tried to smile at myself in the mirror, but instantly lifted my hand to cover up my mouth shyly. It was a nervous tic I'd had my entire life, and even on a day like this one, I couldn't drop it. I fluffed my fringe out carefully; making sure every strand of hair lay at a perfect angle over my forehead.

"You've got a beautiful smile," my mother chided me. "You should show it off more."

"I'll try," I muttered. All my friends and family said that my smile was my best feature, but I didn't buy it. I thought it made me look awkward, but my mother insisted I had a smile to die for.

"Are you sure you don't want me to give Aryan a call?" She cocked her head at me hopefully. I fought the urge to roll my eyes, but she carried on anyway.

"Your aunty next door said he's a nice boy and he's looking for someone to—"

"I'm fine," I cut her off, not wanting to hear the next word out of her mouth. "Tell aunty-next-door that I'm not looking for anyone at the moment."

My mother raised her eyebrows in that way she had and took a step backwards, as though she expected me to detonate. She raised her hands as she headed back to the kitchen.

"We can't have you living in this house forever, you know," she warned over her shoulder as she vanished once more, and this time I allowed myself to roll my eyes at her ridiculousness.

"I don't want to live in this house forever, trust me," I assured her, but under my breath, knowing that I didn't have time for the argument that would ensue if she heard the talkback I'd just given her. I grabbed my bag, hooked it over my shoulder, and examined myself in the mirror one more time.

I was wearing a crisp, carefully-ironed shirt with a stiff collar that was already beginning to dig into my neck, with black pants and a black blazer that I'd borrowed from my mother from the few years she'd spent working as a secretary before she met my father. I tucked a loose strand of hair behind my ear, even though I knew that the humidity would soon undermine my attempts to look neat and tidy. Kajal, or no kajal? It would just melt off by the time I got to the office anyway, and I didn't want to look like I'd spent the whole bus ride over to the office crying. I went for the door and finally stepped out onto the street, feeling a little uneven as I made my way to the bus stop not far from our house. It was early when I left home, but my new office was all the way on the other side of the city and the last thing I wanted was to turn up late on my first day.

I perched on the seat at the bus stop, glancing around. There was nobody else as far as I could see, which was strange for a workday morning like this. But then, it wasn't like our house was close to anything that people might actually have wanted to get to this time in the morning. We were on the outskirts of the city, far removed from anything actually interesting or exciting. Or at least, that's what going to university had taught me – that and being with Akshay.

I closed my eyes briefly and forced myself to push the thought of him from my head. It didn't work. Akshay was still very much present in the back of my mind, whether I liked it or not, and it didn't help that my mother, my granny, and what felt like half of my family were already insisting that I should find a new man to settle down with. They had a cabal of aunties across the city, each one keeping their eyes peeled for any vaguely eligible man who crossed their path and might have been remotely interested in someone like me. I heard my mother on the phone calls she thought were surreptitious, discussing how "suitable" the latest would-be suitor one of her friends across the city had found for me was. I did my best to ignore her. The last thing on my mind now was marriage, especially after what had happened with Akshay.

We had met through the university, despite my family's best efforts to find someone for me in their inner circle, and had hit it off immediately. Well, he had taken a liking to me, and I had never had a boy that handsome or successful or popular, show an interest in me like that before. He had come to the university to talk about his success in the business world, and all the girls in class had spent most of the time wondering if he was single. He wasn't really my type, but everyone else seemed so taken with him that I found myself swept along with their admiration. He was dressed in an expensive suit and doused in heavy aftershave, his hair cropped short against his head and his chin perfectly shaven. He looked as though he spent a lot of time taking care of his appearance, like it was important to him, and practically every woman in the room seemed to flutter after him every time he opened his mouth. Something about the way he rolled his shoulders back and stood tall and strong and a little cocky got a lot of hearts racing, even if I didn't necessarily see what the fuss was about. And then, to my surprise, after the class was done, he headed straight in my direction and asked to take me out. In retrospect, he probably figured out how insecure I was from the way I kept my head low and focused on taking notes, barely sneaking a look up at him the whole time he was talking. And he probably thought that he could manipulate me into being the kind of woman he thought he wanted. But at the time, I felt romanced and flattered and completely caught off-guard by his attention.

"Take me out?" I blinked back at him, feeling stupid, and ignoring that part of me that was pretty sure this was some kind of cruel joke at my expense. The other women around me froze still, as though none of them could believe I was waiting this long to answer him back. I blinked up at him, opening and closing my mouth. I wasn't that attracted to him, but maybe I was wrong? Maybe I'd regret it if I said no and let this apparent catch slip away?

"On a date," he finished for me, raising an eyebrow and smiling at me condescendingly. He always liked to feel like the cleverest person in the room, even when he was asking out some naïve young nineteen-year-old. I let him whisk me away for an evening, more because my friends would have killed me if I hadn't, and soon enough we were dating. He met my family, and they took one look at his excellent prospects and relative success and gave me their blessing. I met his family too, and they seemed a little less taken with me, but I didn't let it put me off. They were old-fashioned and couldn't get their heads around the fact that I hadn't just gone to university to find a husband, but to get an actual degree of my own. That should have been my first red flag – a nod to the fact that in Akshay's family, women who went after what they wanted with regards to their career were often looked at as an anomaly instead of something to be proud of. My family could be backwards-thinking in some ways, but it had been my mother who'd fiercely defended my right to go get a degree, and she wouldn't have heard anything against it. But I put those little doubts to the back of my mind and focused on enjoying myself with Akshay, as much as I could.

We continued to date, and once in a while I found myself wondering if I was just waiting for someone better to come along. I never acted on those intrusive feelings, and put all my excess energy into my studies. I wanted to prove to myself and to his family that I could have as much value in the workplace as he did; he was working his way up the ranks of a prestigious technology company, and I was proud to be with a man who'd worked so hard to achieve everything he wanted. Yes, that meant that sometimes he could be callous or cruel or dismissive towards me, but I would probably feel the same way if my job was as stressful and high-powered as his. I just wanted to write, as he kept reminding me, and that was a far cry from the effort he put into his work to provide for us in the future. I had to bite my tongue to keep from arguing that I would be able to provide for myself in the future, thank you very much, but I knew that a lot of his identity was wrapped up in that job and it never seemed the right time to lay down my own future when his was already unfolding right in front of us. Sometimes, I'd look at my friends and the casual, fun relationships they'd engage in with boys of their own age, and wonder if I was missing out on something I would never be able to get back.

He proposed to me at my graduation ceremony. Of course he did. That was the kind of guy he was, one for big, show-off moments that drew all the attention on to him even when it was meant to be on someone else. He did it at a meal our families were having together, and soon all the talk of the day shifted from the fact that I had just graduated with a degree in journalism near the top of my class to the fact that I was going to marry a successful young man. I still remember that feeling, as he looked up at me from the spot he'd taken on his knee on the restaurant floor, the flickering panic that passed over my brain as I attempted to figure out if there was any way I could say no and not ruin the day for everyone, including myself. Failing to come with a decent solution, I accepted. I didn't feel a lot as the room erupted with excitement around me, as Akshay got to his feet and kissed me on the cheek, but I told myself that I was just in shock. Even though we'd been seeing each other for a long time now, it still felt too soon. I wondered if it ever wouldn't.

That had only been a few months ago. He had been so sure of me then, so certain that we would spend our lives together, and I had done my best to get on board with that line of thought. My mother started planning the wedding almost right away, even though I told her I didn't want to get married too soon. Soon enough, the plans were entirely out of my hands, and I was left wandering aimlessly for the summer after my graduation as

I tried to find a job and avoid letting my mother pin me down on a specific date to build the wedding week around. Since Akshay's family were so well-off, my mother was making the most of the cash attached to the wedding and was planning an affair so lavish that the women at the beauty parlour would be begging her for details for weeks.

And honestly, I was sure I would have gone along with it. I wouldn't have backed out of it, I wouldn't have walked away from it, and all because I was so utterly and completely sure that I really did love Akshay. He was tall, handsome, charming, and could be sweet, given the right set of circumstances. I wasn't sure what else was out there – I had never really had a chance to look – and knowing that I would have a marriage on lockdown only a year or two out of the university was comforting. It meant I could focus my attention on my career without my family offering me up every man they came across as a potential husband. All that was wrapped up in Akshay, in what he represented, and I found myself growing more and more attached to the idea of what life could be like if the two of us were to just get married.

And then, of course, the bad times started to come. Because Akshay hadn't bothered to discuss what he actually expected from a wife with me before he proposed, we had to figure all that out between the two of us in the weeks that followed our engagement. It started when I was putting in some applications for jobs I thought looked interesting across the city, and he walked in on me and looked over my shoulder to see what I was doing on my laptop.

"What are you up to?" He asked, the smell of his aftershave wrapping around me and filling my head.

"Applying for jobs," I replied, glancing up at him, suppressing a little kneejerk of annoyance at his intrusion.

"You know that you won't have to work once we're married, don't you?" He stepped away from me and went to grab something to eat from the kitchen. He had his own flat – minimalist, glossy and perfectly put-together. I hoped that he would let me decorate a little once I moved in, but I had a feeling that he was going to make it hard for me.

"I know I won't have to," I replied, sighing as I pulled my hair into a knot at the top of my head.

"You can write at home," he suggested. "You won't need to go to an office and do it. You'll need a hobby, after all."

I tightened my lips and decided that it was best not to correct him. I didn't want a hobby. I wanted a career. I had wanted to write for my entire life, and I wasn't going to let him talk me out of it just because he thought I would be better off sitting at home, finally learning to cook, after all these years.

I applied, and applied, and applied, and finally, *finally*, I got a reply. It was from the New Delhi Chronicle. I had read these chronicles avidly for years, admiring their reporting on international news and their incisive editorials on topics that interested me. I had only really applied to them on a whim, on the off-chance, and here they were, pulling me in to interview for the position of assistant reporter.

Akshay didn't approve. He obviously thought that I wasn't going to get anywhere in my attempts to find a job and was clearly disgruntled when I actually did. He didn't need to say anything – every time I brought up the interview or my excitement about it, he would sigh softly and drift off and clearly lose any interest in the conversation we were having. In fact, that was happening more and more. Every time we spoke, there was more of a disconnect between us, and even our conversations were becoming fewer and farther between. He would spend more and more time at work and cancel our plans whenever he could get away with it. I was too focused on my interview with The Chronicle to find much time to care.

The interview came and went, and a week or so later, I heard that I had got the job. I was stunned, nervous, thrilled and full of disbelief that my hard work finally seemed to have actually paid off. I was with my mother when I heard the news, and she squeezed my hand and looked at me with a mixture of trepidation and joy in her eyes.

"Are you sure this is the right choice?" She frowned. I blinked at her, not putting the pieces together.

"What do you mean?" I asked her.

"Will you have time for Akshay? And for the wedding?" She got to her feet and stirred the pot that had been sitting simmering on the stove all day. "I need to teach you to cook. And if you want to have children—"

"I don't know yet," I cut her off. I knew she was right, that I hadn't given any thought to how this would affect my relationship with Akshay, but he knew how hard I had to work to be a success. He would understand, if anyone would not, just how important this was to me. Maybe we could push the wedding back a little, have children a little later. We could find a way to make this work. He loved me. I loved him. That was all that really mattered.

Or at least, that's what I kept telling myself. Even after his mother took me aside and implored me to turn down the job so

I could be the wife and mother she knew I could be. I ignored her, knowing that she was from a different generation, knowing that she only meant the best. It wasn't until Akshay was the one suggesting the same thing to me that I started getting worried. But I took the job anyway. I knew I'd regret it if I turned it down. And what was he going to do, dump me if I did what I wanted? He had proposed to me. He wanted to marry me. He wanted us to be together forever. If he left me over this, then everything he'd said to me up until that point had been a lie.

Of course, I should have seen it coming, but that didn't stop it coming as an enormous shock when he broke things off with me. He seemed oddly distant and distracted when he delivered the news, even though it came as a sucker punch to my stomach and left me clutching the back of one of his sleek, expensive chairs just to keep myself standing upright.

"You're ending things?" I whispered, repeating the question for what must have been the half-dozenth times.

"Yes, can't you get it through your head?" He snapped, pacing back and forth. "I don't want to be with you anymore. I don't—"

He stopped abruptly, as though realizing what he was about to say would land him in trouble. He closed his mouth, avoiding my gaze, and I felt tears welling up in my eyes. I wasn't sure if I had entirely liked Akshay, but I had loved him, and he had just ripped out all the security and safety that the proposal had offered out from under my feet. I felt as though my world had been tipped on to its side and I was struggling to keep myself upright.

"Is it because of the job?" I forced myself to look up at him, the tears finally welling over and coursing down my cheeks. "Is it because of that?"

"You're too focused on your career," he shook his head, a flash of anger passing over his face. "I need a wife who's going to care more about what's happening at home than at her office."

He waved his hand dismissively, and I felt a surge of anger course through my veins at the way he said that, as though it was the worst thing I could have done.

"You met me at university," I shot back. "What did you think? That I was just doing it for show?"

"Your career…" he shook his head and sighed deeply, running his fingers through his hair. "It's just writing. It's just words. You don't need to waste your life chasing that."

"I can't believe…" I trailed off and tried to find the words to express the betrayal that felt as though it was about to sweep me off my feet like a tidal wave.

"You should leave." He gestured towards the door. "I'll send your things over when I get the chance."

"Fine," I mustered up some actual anger and grabbed my coat, pulling it over my shoulders and turning away from him so that he couldn't see the devastation in my face.

I walked out of that flat and out of his life and into a new existence that didn't involve Akshay, a wedding and family. The new job started a month later, and I was glad to have something to focus my time and energy towards – even if it didn't keep my family off my back.

They had been so certain about Akshay. They had been more certain about Akshay than I was. When my father found out the reason for his ending our relationship, he took me aside and seriously suggested that I think about turning down the job in order to get him back into my life.

"You want me to give up everything I've been working towards to appease a man who won't give up anything for me?" I widened my eyes at him.

"Give it some thought," my father placed his hand on my shoulder and squeezed comfortingly. He nodded seriously. "If your mother had tried something like this, I don't know if I would have married her."

I glared at him and headed to my room, resisting the urge to slam the door behind me like a furious teenager. Because I knew that even if I were to give up the job, give up my career, pretend I never got my degree and that all I wanted was to be a docile little wife and mother for Akshay, he wouldn't take me back. Because he would know that somewhere deep inside me, there was an urge to do something more, and he would never take that. He needed someone who existed only to serve him and his life and his wants and his needs. I couldn't do that. I never would.

Still, even knowing that, I was heartbroken by the cruel way he brought our relationship to an end. He had been a given part of my life for years now, and my entire world would need time to right itself as I tried to figure out what I wanted. I laser-focused on the job and ignored my aunties across the city who seemed determined to find me someone else to marry, like they could fill the space my life just like that. But I didn't want it to get filled. I wanted to focus on my job, on my life, on what I could build myself that didn't involve a husband or a family. And no one around me seemed to be able to get their head around that fact.

Suddenly, I was pulled out of the in-depth flashback that my brain had inflicted on me and found myself at that bus stop. The sun was rising high above me, and I already knew that I had made the right decision not putting on kajal that morning. I prayed that I would get one of the buses with air conditioning; my hair wouldn't last much longer in this humidity, and I didn't want to turn up on my first day looking like I'd been dragged through the city for it. Those surface-level worries were enough to keep my mind off the feelings deep in my soul, that odd emptiness that I wasn't sure how to fill. If I couldn't have the domesticated life that my family seemed so certain would fulfil me, then I would make sure that I had the career I wanted.

The bus arrived – with AC, much to my relief – and I was whisked across town to the office. I looked around the commuters who filled the streets everywhere I saw, the people in smart suits on expensive phones who didn't seem to have a moments' time to spare, to even glance up from what they were doing. I couldn't keep the smile off my face. This was going to be me. I was going to have a career, an actual job of my own. I would be busy and focused and passionate. Everything I'd worked for while I'd been at university, it was all coming to a head right there and right then. And there was nothing that some silly Akshay led-off engagement could do to keep me from enjoying it. At least that's what I kept telling myself.

I arrived outside the office and looked up at the building towering above me. It was oddly old-fashioned in the street full of offices that looked as though they were so far on the cutting edge, I could have pricked my finger on them, and I liked that. The Chronicle was a real establishment, the kind of place that had decades of history behind it, the kind of place all my old classmates had been beyond jealous to see that I'd landed a job. I quickly fumbled in my bag to pull out the temporary pass I'd received through the mail a few weeks ago and pressed it against the scanner next to the door. It paused for a moment before it beeped obediently, and for the split-second before it went through I felt a surge of panic as I feared that this had all been some horrible joke at my expense.

The door clicked open and I stepped into the building, letting out an internal sigh of relief. I needed to stop treating everything like it was out to get me. This was my achievement and my career, and I was going to savour every second of it.

"Hello, Prisha Laghari?" I nodded towards the receptionist, an older woman who reminded me of my mother. She glanced at a computer screen in front of her, sitting silently for a moment before she responded.

"Straight up to the fourth floor," she gestured towards the lift opposite us, offering me the briefest of smiles, and I bowed my head in thanks and did as I was told. Taking a deep breath, I pressed the button for the lift doors and they slid open with a slight grinding. I stepped inside and was whisked upward towards my future.

Moments later, I was standing in the office of Priya Patel, editor for The Chronicle. She got to her feet as I entered the room and offered me a broad, welcoming, slightly crooked smile. She was wearing a suit that was somehow discreet and ridiculously glamorous at the same time, and put her hand out to shake mine.

"It's good to meet you," she nodded towards a seat on the opposite side of her desk. "We're very pleased to have you working with us."

"Thank you for the opportunity," I replied, managing a smile. I hadn't interviewed with her, and it was a little overwhelming to be in her presence, after all this time reading work that she wrote and commissioned and directed. I eyed the chair she was sitting in. If I could get anywhere close to her position over the course of my career, I would consider it the ultimate victory. I perched on the edge of my seat, clutching my bag on my lap protectively, as though it was a suit of armour.

"So, let's run down what you'll be doing here," she glanced at her watch. "I have a meeting with our investors in a half an hour."

I smiled and felt myself relax into my seat. Here she was, a success, brilliant and intelligent and totally in-control. And if she could do it, then I could do it too.

She went through everything that I'd be expected to take on while I was here. I had read the job post at least a dozen times through to commit every word to memory, so none of it was new to me, but it was good to hear it again anyway. Mostly, I'd be doing supplemental reporting work, fact-checking and proof-reading and lots of other grunt work that needed to get done around the office. For some people – for people like Akshay – it probably would have seemed painfully dull, but to me, it was unimaginably exciting. It was the start of something – the beginning. It was far too thrilling to be dull.

Priya pointed me in the direction of my desk, and I sank down into the threadbare chair and booted up the hopelessly out-of-date computer to sign in to my account. I paused for a moment, staring off into space, a smile curling up on to my lips. This was actually happening. I was actually here. I couldn't believe it.

Suddenly, my gaze was drawn by movement; a man had just walked into the room, into my line of sight. I blinked twice and my vision focused on him, and for a moment, my heart stopped.

It felt as though I had seen him before, even though that was impossible. He stood a good few inches taller than me, with broad shoulders that tapered down into a slim waist, his body lean and toned in a way that his expensive shirt couldn't disguise. A swoop of thick, dark hair draped down over his forehead, the same colour as his dark-chocolate eyes. There was a smattering of stubble over his sharp jaw, and I found myself fighting the urge to run my hands over it, to feel the roughness of it beneath my fingertips. His eyes swept around the room commandingly as he placed a hand on the back of a chair and frowned slightly, and suddenly, I realized that his gaze had fallen on me. And there I was, sitting there with my lips slightly parted and my heart finally remembering to beat again after what felt like a full minute of nothing but him.

I shifted in my seat and cleared my throat, returning my attention to the screen in front of me, but I could still feel the man's eyes on me. I swallowed heavily and forced myself to keep my focus on the computer. The last thing I needed was to be caught ogling one of my new colleagues, especially on my first day. Even if he did remind me of some movie star I distantly remembered from years ago, someone I'd spent hours poring over a single video of until it wore out when I was too young to realize exactly why I wanted to look at him so badly. Maybe that's where I thought I recognised him from. Or maybe it was something more than that.

"Hey!" A perky voice from behind drew my attention, and I turned to find myself faced with a woman a few years older than me, wearing a bright orange shirt and an even brighter smile.

"You must be Prisha," she greeted me with a cocked head and a nod. "You've just started here, haven't you?"

"That's right," I replied, returning her smile and dragging my eyes from the gorgeous guy as best I could.

"Good to meet you," she thrust her hand in my direction and I took it. "I'm Anika."

"Nice to meet you," I replied, grateful for how friendly she was being, because I had a habit of vanishing into the background around people I didn't know. I took a hesitant breath, and then nodded in the direction of the man who'd just entered the room.

"Do you...do you have any idea who that is?" I asked and Anika glanced up and cocked an eyebrow.

"That's Rajesh," she rolled her eyes, as though even his name was enough to get her hackles up. "Don't worry; you'll get to know him soon. He won't let anyone get away with not knowing him." She continued.

"Oh, okay," I replied vaguely, turning my attention back to him. Rajesh. It was a name I'd heard a thousand times before, but suddenly it seemed to hold some sort of charm, like a spell I could use to summon him.

"Anyway, Priya asked me to show you around," Anika jerked her head towards the rest of the office. "Come on, let me give you the tour."

"Sounds good," I agreed, and got to my feet, ignoring the pull in my stomach that seemed intent on dragging me towards Rajesh, and focusing in on making a good impression on my first day of work.

Two weeks into my contract at The Chronicle, and it was finally starting to feel like home. I strode in there every morning, feeling like the coolest kid of the block, past scores of people hurrying to their own offices. I would rehearse little dialogues in my head, trying to sound casual as I made my way into the office – *oh, yeah, I work at The Chronicle. I'm a journalist.*

It still felt odd to be able to think those words and know they were true. I had spent so long building myself up to this, working my backside off to land here, and now that I had arrived, it felt almost surreal. But with every passing day, every proofread and fact-check that landed on my desk, I felt more and more like I belonged here. That was, until I saw Rajesh again.

I hadn't laid my eyes on him since that first day, even though I had thought about him plenty lot. He had a presence around the office, even when he wasn't here. He'd been away for two weeks covering something abroad, and people seemed both relieved and dismayed that he was out of the office for so long.

The whispers around him fascinated me, even if that first glimpse of him hadn't done enough. The way people spoke about him, he sounded as though he was both the best possible person to work with and a nightmare to keep on track. He had come in to the office when he was twenty-one, with no formal education but several years proving himself covering local news back in his hometown. He dropped all that to come out here as soon as he got the chance, sensing a bigger fish to fry, and had thrown himself at his work with a crazy efficiency that the rest of the office seemed to talk about with something close to awe. He was regularly travelling the world to nail down the best and most interesting stories, and he was one of The Chronicle's most notorious reporters, especially when it came to getting the facts out of tricky interview subjects. He sounded like the exact kind of reporter I wanted to be one day, and yet, people still seemed a little unnerved by him. And it wasn't until I met him again that I realized why.

I was making myself a tea to take back to my desk to get me through that mid-morning slump when he wandered into the break room, out of nowhere. I had no idea he'd returned from his trip abroad, and my jaw dropped as soon as he walked in. He looked even better than he had the last time I'd seen him, if that was even possible. This time, I had everything I'd been told about him crowding my head on top of my initial attraction, and it left me gaping at him like a guppy fish as he went about getting himself something to drink.

"Hi. Sorry," I blurted out. "I'm Prisha. I'm new. I don't think we've met."

He glanced up at me briefly, eyes travelling up and down my body in a way that made me flush. His expression didn't change one bit.

"No, I don't think we have," he conceded, and finished making himself a cup of tea.

"I've heard a lot about your work," I went on, knowing that I was burbling and should have shut my mouth, but finding myself unable.

"Right," he replied, and it was just an acknowledgement of what I'd said to him as opposed to an attempt to get the conversation going. I looked down at my tea and took a deep breath.

"I look forward to working with you," I managed, the words sounding almost comically formal as they came out of my mouth.

"Sure," he turned away from me, taking his tea and vanishing back out into the office space outside. I blinked at him a couple of times as he walked away. Was it something I'd done? The rest of the office had been incredibly welcoming and supportive over the time that I'd been here, and now he was just… walking away? Like I was nothing? Maybe he didn't realize that I was actually working on the newspaper. Maybe he thought I was the trolley lady or something like that, or here to clean up. I took my tea and headed back to my desk, and decided to give him the benefit of doubt for the time being. He was probably just jet-lagged from spending too much time travelling. There was nothing more to read into it than that. Or at least that's what I told myself after the first time.

After the second time we met, he was equally as dismissive and rude to me, and I found myself bristling at him. He didn't need to be that way. No one was making him. And yet, here he was, acting nothing but an asshole and not giving much of a damn how I felt about it. He wasn't cruel to me as much as he was just outright ignoring my presence in the office. At first, I thought it might just have been because he was so focused in his work and didn't have time to bother making new friends at work, but I saw him laughing and joking with other members of the staff who weren't me. He would shut down as soon as I tried to join the conversation, even if the person he was talking to was happy to see me. He didn't say anything awful to me – in fact, the problem lay more in what he didn't say, the way he glanced away from me when I spoke, and the way his eyes drifted off when he did look at me. It made me self-conscious in a way I'd never been before. It was the last thing I needed at this office, to be feeling this insecure about myself and I soon found myself avoiding him like the plague. I didn't want myself to bother with him if he was just going to treat me that poorly. I had work to be getting on with, and besides, he was out of the office so much that I wouldn't have to deal with him that much in the future. I probably wouldn't see anything of him.

I swear, it must have been moments after those words crossed my mind that I got called into Priya's office. Like I had tempted fate by letting them so much as cross my mind. I stood in front of her desk, shifting back and forth from one foot to the other nervously. She had mostly communicated with me by email since I had arrived, and I had a feeling that being asked to see her in person probably wasn't an overly good sign. I tucked a loose strand of hair behind my ear and found that my fingers were trembling a little. *Get it together, Prisha.*

"Prisha, thanks for coming in," Priya nodded to one of two chairs on the opposite side of her desk. There had only been one when I'd come in on my first day. Was someone else joining us?

"Sorry about the delay," she sighed, glancing at her watch. "He's never been great with time-keeping—"

The door burst open behind me, and I turned to find Rajesh standing there. He was wearing a pale blue shirt that was rolled up past his elbows once more, and I found my eyes drifting towards his strong hands and deft fingers. I had spotted him typing a few times, that little furrow in his brow as his fingers flew across the keyboard, and I had to admit it was pretty hot seeing him at work like that. I let out a small, internal sigh as soon as I laid eyes on him. Of course he was the one in here with me as though I wasn't nervous or uncomfortable enough.

"Sorry I'm late," he raked his fingers through his thick hair and took a seat next to me. He could do with a trim; if my mother had laid eyes on him, the first thing she would do would have him sit down in a chair in our kitchen with a towel draped around his shoulders so she could get him looking a bit more professional.

"No problem," Priya glanced at me, acknowledging his lateness with one of those glances that only women share with one another. "There's something I need to talk to you both about."

Rajesh and I looked over at one another, and it was clear that the same thought was going through both our minds – what in goodness name could she have to talk to us about that involved both of us? We'd barely been in the same room these last few weeks.

"Rajesh, it's about your trip next week," she began, clasping her hands on the desk in front of her. He raised his eyebrows and leaned back.

"To the business conference in Bengaluru?" He cocked an eyebrow.

"That's the one." She nodded. "Natalie has pulled out."

"Really?" He sounded pissed. "Why? What happened?"

"Death in the family," Priya replied gravely. "She'll be out for a few weeks, sends her apologies."

"So what, I'm just going by myself now?" He crossed his arms over his chest. "There won't be enough time to do everything—"

"No, you're not," she cut him off. "You're going with Prisha."

"What?" I exclaimed, unable to keep quiet any longer. Rajesh opened his mouth in surprise.

"What are you talking about?" He shook his head, as though the very thought was unthinkable.

"You need someone to go down with you to keep you in check," Priya nodded towards me. Rajesh snorted.

"To keep me in check?" He shot back incredulously. "Are you serious? With all due respect, she's been here—"

"She's been here long enough for me to know that I trust her with this," Priya cut him off again, and he sat back in his seat with a small sigh. It was obvious that he respected her and, perhaps more importantly, that he knew there was no chance of talking her out of this because she was the one in charge. I sat there, staring at her, trying to make any kind of sense of what had just happened.

"You want me to go with you?" I looked over at Rajesh, and he raked his fingers through his hair once more, obviously put out.

"I don't," he shot back, and my stomach tightened. I hated feeling unwanted.

"But you're going," Priya gave him a hard look that told me that she wasn't going to let him make me uncomfortable. "Prisha, is that okay with you? Can you go?"

"How long will it be for?" I asked, ignoring the waves of anger wafting from the man sitting beside me. "And when do we leave?"

"Two weeks, and Monday," she replied. "We'll send you along an itinerary. Does that work for you?"

"No problem," I nodded firmly. "Thank you for the opportunity."

"Don't make me regret it," Priya cocked an eyebrow at me, and even though her voice was pleasant, I could tell that she was warning me not to let her down. "Now, I need to talk with Rajesh. Thanks for your time."

I got to my feet, nodding to both politely, and then headed back to my desk. I took a seat back at my desk, stared at my screen blankly for a second, and then what had just happened actually began to sink in.

She had picked me. She had chosen me, out of everyone else in that office, to travel with him to that conference, and judging by what everyone had told me, working with him was one of those hallowed honours that was only bestowed on the… well, the most worthy? The most willing? The one most likely to follow what Priya told me to do because I was still so in awe of her? Yes, it was probably that last one, now that I thought of it. But still. I'd be working with a journalist known across the city – across the country. I would take it. Even if it meant spending two weeks alone with Rajesh.

Alone? With Rajesh? Now that it was sinking in, I had no idea how to feel about it. Part of me was utterly and completely dreading it already. I wasn't sure that I could take two whole weeks of his dismissive attitude and his sighs and his utter laser-focus on nothing but work. But then, on the other hand…

What if he started to see me differently? Think of what it could do for me. For my career. I hastily reminded myself that this was what I should be worried about, instead of wondering how his hands would have felt tracing over my skin instead of a keyboard. I shoved the thought angrily from my brain; the last thing I needed was to get distracted by the fact I was going to be alone with a handsome man for a couple of weeks. I was a grown-up woman and I wasn't going to let some silly little crush – that was probably just a rebound anyway – get in the way of what could be an amazing career opportunity for me.

My head still spinning, I focused my energy back on work, putting on the front of someone industrious and focused. But everything that was to come was ticking away at the back of my mind, and I couldn't wait to see what I was right about.

I let out a long sigh and settled into my seat. It had been a nightmare fighting through everyone at the airport to get to where we needed to be, but we were finally on the plane to Mumbai and I was about to take on the biggest two weeks of my career to date. I looked out of the window, and caught a dim view of my own reflection smiling back excitedly.

And then, Rajesh took his seat next to me, and my good mood vanished just like that to be replaced with a skittish nervousness that seemed to overwhelm me every time I was around him. I shifted in my seat, crossing and uncrossing my legs, and he glanced up at me.

"Are you alright?" He asked, his voice a little terse. I nodded.

"I'm fine," I replied, trying to keep the discomfort that must have been written on my face out of my voice. "Thank you."

"Welcome," he grunted back at me, and pulled out his laptop and placed it on the table in front of his seat. I saw him as he booted up his computer, that little furrow between his brows appearing once more. That seemed to happen a lot when I was around.

It had been a hectic few days, as I tried to convince my mother that going away for a couple of weeks with this man on a work trip didn't mean I had to introduce him to the family first, but I was finally here and I couldn't believe it was really happening. Priya, as I had suspected, had assigned me to Rajesh to keep an eye on him and make sure that he didn't go off on any tangents that wouldn't reflect well on The Chronicle. And just before we left the office to go for the plane, she pulled me aside.

"Don't worry about Rajesh," she waved a hand in the direction of where he was standing, his bags placed at his feet and his smart jacket pulled haphazardly over his shoulders. "He's like this with everyone, at first. It gets better, trust me."

"I hope so," I smiled nervously, and glanced over at him. He was clean-shaven, his hair brushed back from his face, and he looked like the kind of man my mother would want me to bring home to her. Priya paused for a moment, then cocked her head at me and spoke slowly.

"You know about the relationships clause in the contract, don't you?" She looked at me intently. I stared back at her blankly. So much had happened since I'd signed those contracts, I'd forgotten practically everything that was in them.

"There are no inter-colleague romantic relationships allowed here," she explained quickly.

"Oh, of course," I nodded, and wondered why she was telling me this. Was my attraction towards Rajesh that obvious? I had no idea whether I should have been offended by what she was saying, or just take it as a friendly warning.

"Good," she patted me on the arm, and then waved me towards the door. "Go, you don't want to be late for the plane!"

Rajesh had avoided me since he'd heard that we were going to be spending the next two weeks together. I couldn't say I blamed him. He was used to working with highly experienced colleagues he got on well with, and here I was, a complete newbie who he seemed to actively disdain most of the time. Of course he wasn't happy about this. But he was stuck with me, like it or not, and he was going to have to make the best of the situation.

Our knees touched briefly across the seats, and I felt a jolt of electricity pass from his body to mine. I jumped slightly, making the table shake, and clamped my feet to the ground. He shot me an irritated look.

"Sorry," I muttered, and he shrugged and focused his attention back to the computer in front of him. I pressed my head to the cool glass as the plane pulled down the runway, and I felt that flicker of excitement pricks up in me once more.

I still wasn't entirely sure why someone like Rajesh would want to cover a business conference like this one. He had been more inclined towards hard news and was best known for chasing down strong political stories, for uncovering corruption wherever it hid, and this conference was really just a chance for various businesses to show off their wares and see what their competitors were up to. It didn't seem like the kind of place he would willingly put himself in, and I wondered again if that was why Priya had sent me. If I was aware of it, then there was no doubt that she was too. There was something else going on here and I was going to find it out.

I closed my eyes and drifted off to sleep. I had slept poorly the night before, tossing and turning and thinking about what it would be like to be alone with Rajesh for so long, and then getting annoyed at myself for letting my brain stray in that direction. It seemed like something deep inside me desperately wanted me to make a damn fool of myself in front of this man, to have me pining over him like a teenager with her first crush, and I wasn't going to give in to it, especially not when he was being so rude to me.

I woke with a start, and my eyes flew open to be greeted by the brightness of the mid-day sun pouring through the window beside me. I lifted my head from the glass, and surreptitiously checked to make sure that I hadn't drooled in my sleep. I might not have been indulging my crush, but the last thing I wanted was for a respected colleague like Rajesh to see me looking like I'd just climbed out of bed.

"Excuse me?" A voice came from beside me; the same voice that I assumed had woken me up. I turned to find myself facing a slim, young woman with a tight smile who was holding out a small package in my direction. I took it – it was warm and wrapped in foil, and it took me a minute to realize that this trip came with a meal as part of the ticket price.

"Oh, thank you," I smiled up at her, stifling a yawn. She handed a package to Rajesh, who was completely lost in his work, and he lifted his head and offered her a dazzling smile that I wasn't aware till that moment that he was even capable of. I felt a twinge of jealousy. What had she done to earn it that I hadn't? I quickly stamped down my irrational reaction and began peeling back the foil from my food and grabbed the small plastic cutlery set that came with it. My stomach grumbled as the rich, savoury aroma hit me – and then my heart sank.

I didn't want to make a fuss, so I quietly picked out the mutton from the biryani and piled it up on a napkin next to me.

But, to my dismay, it seemed thoroughly mixed through. I didn't eat meat, and even the sight of it was making me a little queasy, but the last thing I wanted was to make some big deal about not being catered to.

"What are you doing?" Rajesh asked, his mouth half-full, as he watched me deconstruct my food to try and get out all the meat.

"I'm a vegetarian," I replied, and he cocked his head at me and sat silently for a moment, as though I'd actually managed to present him with a conundrum he didn't immediately have an answer to.

"Didn't you order the vegetarian meal?" He asked.

"I'm certain I did, but it's okay," I shrugged. "I don't want to make a fuss."

He stared at me for another moment, and then got to his feet and vanished off down the aisle, leaving me sitting there alone once more. I raised my eyebrows, irritated. Well, if that was how he was going to be about it.

I continued methodically removing the meat from my meal, and a few minutes later, Rajesh returned. I looked up and found him proffering another tinfoil package in my direction. I took it, unwrapped it, and found it mercifully free of meat.

"Did you—"

"I couldn't have you going hungry," he shrugged. "I need you working at your highest capacity."

I might have been wrong, but I was pretty sure that I saw the flicker of a smile pass over his face. It was the first one that I had seen aimed in my direction from him, and it made my heart lurch up in my chest.

"Thanks," I smiled back, and he nodded, sliding into his seat. I tucked in – for pre-packaged food, it wasn't bad, and I was glad to have something to eat that I could actually enjoy without reserve. Rajesh didn't immediately grab for his laptop, and instead cocked his head at me and watched me as I ate.

"What is it?" I asked nervously, covering my mouth to make sure I wasn't spraying food everywhere.

"Nothing," he shook his head, and glanced out the window. "Huh, it's been a long time since I went to Mumbai."

"You've been there before?"

"Years ago," he nodded, still peering out of the window as though there was something out there that fascinated him. "I was covering a story for the elections. It was one of the first stories I ever did for The Chronicle, actually."

"That must have been a while ago," I replied without thinking, and instantly cursed myself internally. Because obviously, the best way to get into his good graces was by calling him old. To my relief, he grinned in amusement as my face flushed bright red.

"I'm not that ancient," he teased, and leaned forward for a moment – then seemed to force himself back against the seat, frowning once more, all the light that had appeared vanishing at once from his face. It was like he was trying to stifle it, and I had no idea why he would want to do that since his face was so gloriously full of life when he spoke the way he did.

"I know, I know," I replied. "So, what's the story you're following at this conference?"

He didn't reply for a moment, and instead eyed me for a split second. I could see something on his face, an expression that passed fleetingly over his features, only to vanish a moment later. Like he was considering something, but decided against it.

"I just think it's good to check in with these kinds of businesses once in a while," he responded, speaking a little slower than before, as though he was picking his words carefully. "And usually something interesting comes up while I'm down there."

"Fair enough," I replied, meeting his gaze steadily to let him know that I was pretty sure he was trying to fool me and that I wasn't going to fall for it that easily. "It just seems a little outside your realm of interest, that's all."

"Everything is within my realm of interest," his eyes flashed at me for a moment, and I stopped eating. I stopped breathing. Just once in a while, he would catch me off-guard in a way that left me feeling as though my insides were curling up into smoke. It was a sensation that I was getting addicted to, and I knew I had to shake my dependence before it became a problem.

"So, what about you?" He asked, clearly attempting to switch the subject to something he found more palatable. I wasn't going to stop him. I had the feeling that forcing the truth out of him was only going to end with him hating me more than he already seemed to, and I wasn't interested in finding out how that felt. I swallowed, took a deep breath, and felt my heart stutter back into life once more.

"What about me?" I asked evasively. I was still curious to see what he was hiding from me, and now the two of us were locked in this conversational dance where we were both trying to throw off the other's suspicions about our intentions.

"What's your…" He waved his hand expressively. "Realm of interest?"

"Anything that The Chronicle wants me to do," I replied at once, and he flicked his eyes up as though asking the gods for patience.

"You must have something in particular you like," he pointed out patiently. "Something you find... interesting, something that excites you."

His eyes flicked for a split second down to my lips, and then back up to meet my gaze. Was he doing that to throw me off? Or was there something more to it?

"If I could write about anything..." I trailed off, scrambling to find a good answer. I had thought about this so often that it felt as though there was almost too much to condense into one brief answer: I wanted to write about everything and anything, and nothing felt as though it was enough to box me in.

"I would write about everything," I raised my eyebrows at him, daring him to challenge me on what I'd just said. A smile curled up on to his lips, and he seemed satisfied with the answer I offered him.

"That's how I felt when I was your age," he nodded. "You'll find your specialties eventually, but you should never forget how it feels to want to cover everything you can get your hands on."

"I have to admit, I didn't necessarily have business conferences in mind when I started working for Priya," I admitted jokingly.

"Me neither," he leaned in, as though he was sharing a secret with me. "But trust me, there are so many good stories there. So many egos, so many companies – it's fascinating."

"I guess I won't just have to take your word for it," I remarked playfully and realized, with a start, that I was flirting with him.

I wasn't good at flirting, never had been, Akshay had been the one to come on to me and do all the chasing, but there was no doubt that I was enjoying this little back and forth more than professionally. And he seemed to be, too, if his guarded smile was anything to go by. I reminded myself of what Priya had told me before I left – that even if I wanted to; I wasn't allowed to date Rajesh. Not that I wanted to. But still, having my career on the line like that was an excellent deterrent.

"I should get back to work," Rajesh gestured to his laptop, and I nodded, watching him as he ducked his head back down to focus on the screen once more. He must have known that if we kept going down this path, he was going to reveal something he didn't want to, though he would have been crazy to think that I was going to let it go just like that. I placed my head against the glass once more and closed my eyes, letting out a long sigh, and wondered how on earth I was going to get through the next two weeks.

We arrived at the airport in the afternoon the day before the conference, and I was feeling ragged and worn-out from travel. As we waited to pick up our bags and head across to the taxi that was going to take us to the hotel, I found myself eyeing a woman standing about ten metres from me. She must have come off a plane as well, but she looked so pulled-together compared to how I felt. Her hair was pulled back into a neat, high ponytail, her make-up flawless and unsmudged, and her clothes perfectly pressed despite how long she must have spent sitting in a cramped plane seat. Where did she learn to have that kind of poise and grace, and would she be so kind as to share her secret with me?

Rajesh was standing next to me, and idly followed my gaze across the room – and as soon as he saw who I was looking at, he seemed to jolt with surprise.

"Shit," he muttered, and I turned to him, eyes wide.

"What is it?" I asked, looking at the woman once more as though I could figure out what had gotten Rajesh so put out.

"I know her," he sighed, and I looked back at the woman once more.

"How?" I asked, but I was pretty sure I already knew the answer to that question without him having to elaborate any further. He shifted so that his back was to her a little and she couldn't easily make out our faces, like he was avoiding her.

"She's my ex," he muttered, keeping his voice low so as not to alert her to our presence. "Lena. She's a journalist too. She must be here to cover the conference..."

"She's coming over here," I warned him, peering over his shoulder and watching with mild amusement as she got closer. I was so used to seeing Rajesh completely in control that I couldn't help but find it a tiny bit entertaining when he was as flustered as he normally made me feel. The woman approached – she was a little older than me, with dark hair and dark eyes, and our gazes met for a brief second over Rajesh' shoulder. Her eyes flashed with an emotion I couldn't quite put my finger on, and Rajesh let out a sigh and turned around to face her. He plastered a smile over his irritated expression as soon as they were facing each other.

"Lena," he nodded, leaning to peck her on the cheek in greeting and leaving me with a flash of jealousy at their physical ease around each other. "Here for the conference?"

"Of course," she replied. "You too? For The Chronicle?"

"That's right," he nodded. "Who are you covering it for?"

"Pritath Industries," she replied. They were both speaking quickly, as though they were hoping to find some way to catch the other one out. "I'm still freelancing."

"Can't find anywhere to give you a full-time job?" He cocked his head at her, and she rolled her eyes.

"Can't find anywhere that interests me enough to make me want to settle down," she shot back, and finally her gaze travelled to me once more. "And she is?"

"This is Prisha," he glanced in my direction. "She's just started at The Chronicle. She's helping me out over the next couple of weeks."

"I'll bet she is," Lena agreed, looking me up and down. I found myself shifting uncomfortably under her prying eyes, even though I knew that she was just using me as a stick to beat Rajesh with and I shouldn't take it personally. But there was something about the way she was looking at me – as though she already knew more about me than I would know about myself in a lifetime – that made me want to duck away. I forced myself to meet her gaze and eventually she broke away and turned her attention back to Rajesh.

"I guess I'll see you there, then," she remarked. "Good running into you."

"Whatever you say," Rajesh muttered as he watched her stride away to pick up her bags. I waited till she was out of earshot before I dived in to demand an explanation for what I'd just seen.

"That's your ex?" I asked, and he finally glanced over his shoulder at me, as though he had half-forgotten I was there. The notion was upsetting.

"Yes," he nodded grimly. "We dated for a few months a long time ago, and it… it didn't end well."

"I can tell," I confirmed; the atmosphere between them had been so toxic I was surprised that the airport janitors hadn't arrived to cordon off the area for the safety of the public.

"So, we're going to have her around for the next couple of weeks as well?" I remarked, and he closed his eyes for a moment as though the reality of the situation was only just dawning on him.

"Yes, I suppose we are," he sighed. "Come on, let's get our bags. The hotel's a while away and I want to get to bed for a reasonable time, so we're up bright and early tomorrow."

"So you can beat her to the conference?" I teased. I could see through him. Finally, the briefest smile flickered on his face.

"Yeah, something like that," he agreed, and we waited in companionable silence for our bags to come. I still wasn't sure exactly where we stood, but I knew that he at least liked me better than that ex of his, and right now that was a victory I would take.

It took a while for our bags to come, and by the time they did, the taxi that had been called for us had presumably grown bored and driven off, leaving us to hail down our own transport across the city to the hotel. I peered out of the window with a big grin on my face as we drove. I had spent my whole life in Delhi, and finally finding myself somewhere new was more exciting than I had thought it would be. I wanted to play it cool in front of Rajesh, but I couldn't hide my excitement. And, if anything, he seemed to find my thrill in the face of a whole new place entertaining.

"You know we won't be seeing a lot of the city, right?" He reminded me. "We'll mostly be spending all our time at the conference."

"I know," I assured him. "That's why I'm taking it all in now. I know Mum is going to ask about it when I get back."

"Mine always tries to get me to take pictures," he remarked. "And I have to remind her that most of the time people don't actually want me covering their businesses, and taking pictures like a tourist is just going to attract attention."

"I didn't even think of that," I murmured, half to myself. And then I turned to him. "But you don't care who knows you're at this conference, do you? Because you're just covering the conference?"

"Yes, that's right," he nodded, but he slid his eyes away from mine as though he couldn't look me in the eye and say it. I pressed my lips together. There was something more going on here, and I would get to the bottom of it, no matter how hard he tried to keep me at arm's length.

We arrived at the hotel, and I climbed out of the taxi while Rajesh paid and got the receipt to add to our expenses and stood in front of the place that I'd be calling home for the next couple of weeks. I had seen places like this before, but never thought for a second I would actually be in one. The building was huge, towering above us so far I was surprised it didn't vanish into the clouds, and perfectly sleek, the outside punctuated by a few strips of pale blue light that spelled out the name of the company that owned the building down the side. The lobby looked warm and inviting, and I tugged my coat around my shoulders, not realizing until that moment that I was actually cold.

"Come on, let's get our rooms," Rajesh was suddenly beside me, and his hand was on the small of my back. I jumped, not expecting his touch. He pulled his hand away at once.

"Sorry, a force of habit," he shrugged, as though it was nothing, and I blinked at him a couple of times as I waited for my heart rate to return to normal.

"Right," I nodded, and let him lead me into the lobby of the hotel.

He headed straight for the reception desk, which was staffed by a pretty girl a few years younger than me. She beamed so widely when he approached, I thought she might pull something. Inside, the hotel was all decked out in preparation for the conference, the entire place dripping with signs and brochures and announcements letting everyone who cared to know what was going to happen over the next couple of weeks. I perched myself nervously on the edge of one of the stiff, robin egg blue chairs in the corner of the room, hoping not to draw too much attention for myself or someone, say or do something that would get us in trouble. I closed my eyes briefly, succumbing to the tiredness of travelling all day, but opened once more when I heard Rajesh's raised voice across the room.

"What the hell are you talking about?" He furrowed his brow deeply, and I got up to see what all the fuss was about.

"What's going on?" I asked as I arrived at his elbow. The receptionist, whose smile had been swiftly wiped from her face, turned her attention to me, and it was clear she was making a Herculean effort to keep her voice steady in the face of Rajesh' irritation.

"There was a mix-up," she explained. "We only booked one room for the two of you. A new one will be available tomorrow, but for tonight, the rest of the hotel is entirely booked out."

"Can't I just…" Rajesh waved his hand. "I could bring some sheets down here and sleep on the couches. I don't mind."

"We can't allow you to sleep anywhere other than inside a room, sir," she replied, her voice pointedly neutral. "Fire safety regulations won't allow it."

Rajesh heaved a sigh, his shoulders rising and falling, and he rubbed his hand over his face as though trying to clear the day from his head so he could think straight. Meanwhile, I was standing next to him feeling as though someone had just shifted the ground out from underneath me.

I knew I shouldn't have been excited. I knew I should have been just as irritated as he was at this turn of events. But that didn't mean that I could put a stop to the tiny flicker of thrill that traced up my spine and across my scalp, or hide the little smile that briefly appeared on my face before he turned his attention back to me and I had to swiftly wipe it off.

"I'm sorry about this," he shook his head apologetically. "Just one night? It doesn't look like we've got any options and I need to get some sleep."

"It's okay," I nodded seriously, hoping my face was arranged in a convincingly irritated fashion. "Just for tonight."

"Fine," Rajesh sighed, and held out his hand for the keys. "Let's get our bags up and we can figure out where I can sleep."

We gathered our things and headed up in the lift to our room. I still couldn't believe I could actually call it *our* room, if just for tonight. And yes, it wasn't like he was going to be sliding into the bed next to me, but we'd be sharing a space, the two of us together if only for the next few hours. I knew that I was physically tired, but mentally, it felt as though my brain was bouncing around on fire with excitement.

Rajesh helped me get my bags up to the door, and he unlocked for us; as soon as he stepped inside, he let out a low whistle.

"This place..." he glanced around. "It's not what I expected."

"Oh my goodness," I followed him in, and my eyebrows shot up as I saw where we'd be staying for the night. "This looks..."

The room was huge, with an enormous double bed dominating most of the space. A pair of doors that led to a generous balcony was filtering in a soft, warm glow from the city, and there was a large ensuite bathroom just visible through a cracked-open door next to me. It wasn't exactly the kind of room I'd imagined staying in for a business conference.

"I'll see if I can get some extra covers," he remarked as he dumped the bags next to him. "I'm sorry about all of this. It isn't..."

He trailed off, and for a moment, it was just the two of us, standing there, looking at each other in this room, by ourselves, so far from anything that we might have recognised as our real lives. Sequestered here all alone, the two of us in this bedroom in this hotel in a new city. Everything felt fallow and fresh and I saw his eyes drift downwards to my lips once again. I felt a tug in my belly, one that pulled me a step towards him. He took a breath, and just like that, whatever spell the two of us had been under was broken. It was gone.

"I should get some rest," he sat down on the edge of the bed and pulled off his shoes, stretching. I found myself perching on the other side, deeply aware of how close he was to me and knowing that if I just leaned back a few inches, I could have touched him, could have brushed my fingers across that stubble on his cheek that I had been so desperately aware of from the very first moment I saw him.

But, of course, I didn't. I sat there and stared into space, breathing deeply and quietly and willing my heartbeat to return to normal already. I heard Rajesh let out a small groan and the bed bounced, and I turned to see that he had keeled over where he sat.

"I'm sorry," he mumbled, voice a little dulled by the covers near his mouth. "I'm just so tired..."

Suddenly, I felt a wave of exhaustion wash over me too, and I found myself mirroring his motions, letting myself slip down on to the bed and closing my eyes. Slipping out of my shoes, I tucked my feet below me, and told myself that this would just be for a minute. I could hear his breath softening behind me, turning into something sweeter and gentler as the stress of the day seemed to lift from his shoulders. I yawned and tucked my hands beneath my face to lie down. Just until I was feeling awake enough to walk around again. I wouldn't go to sleep...

I woke the next day slowly. Slowly enough that it took me a while to realize what was happening. Slowly enough that I didn't stop it at once.

His arm was wrapped around my waist, and I was pulled tight against his body. I could feel his breath, steady and warm, against the back of my neck. I smiled, still not conscious enough to make sense of the sensations coursing through my body, but simply knowing that I liked it and I didn't want it to stop. The warmth of his body wrapped around mine, the way his thumb moved steadily up and down my leg where it was resting, as though reassuring me – it had been a long time since I had felt this safe or slept this well, and I didn't want it to end. I was half in a dream, and the strength of his hands on my body was all that kept me tethered to the real world. I closed my eyes and was about to let sleep take me once more – until I realized who I must have been sharing a bed with.

I leaped up, rolling out from beneath the arm tossed across me and landed on my feet on the floor next to the bed. I looked around, reminding myself just where I was – the hotel room, the one they had accidentally assigned to just the two of us. I blinked the sleep from my eyes, and looked down at the bed. Rajesh was still lying there, his body arched in such a way that I knew if I'd wanted to slide back into his arms, I could have done it without disturbing him. He was sleeping peacefully, eyes drifted shut and breath soft as he caught up on his rest. There was something oddly, strangely intimate about seeing him like this – even more intimate than the act of cuddling with him in the bed like I just had been. He was vulnerable, completely, and he had let himself become that way in front of me. My heart flipped up in my chest, and I took a deep breath to steady it. I needed to stay calm. I needed to get any thought of Rajesh and I out of my head for good. And I needed to keep the all-too-vivid memory of his fingers tracing over my thigh out of my brain.

I made my way through to the bathroom, planted my hands on the sink, and looked at myself in the mirror. My hair was messy and I quickly pulled it loose from the tie I had put it in the day before while we had been travelling. Shaking it out, I looked at myself in the mirror, and wanted to curse how stupid I had been to lie in bed with that man and think that I would be able to keep it completely innocent. I had a crush on him, nothing more, but if I continued to indulge in it like this, then it would become something I couldn't control. I was already starting to wonder if it had gotten out of hand, something greater than I could keep to myself.

I climbed into a shower and washed the last twenty-four hours off me – the travel, the room we had to share, the feel of his body curled around mine. Or at least, I tried to. Because getting rid of those thoughts weren't as easy as that.

I wrapped myself in a towel and stepped out to grab my bag. I had forgotten to bring it in and prayed that he was still asleep, but of course, with my luck the last couple of days, his eyes opened as soon as I stepped out of the bathroom.

"Shit, sorry," he averted his eyes as soon as he saw me, looking towards the wall as I hurried to grab my bag. I was so aware of my nakedness beneath the towel, how close I was to being completely nude in front of him. I flushed bright red and ducked back into the bathroom, dressing hurriedly, and when I emerged, I found him dressed in a smart shirt and trousers. He looked good, put-together and professional – far different than the man who had been holding me close just a few minutes before.

"Morning," he nodded at me, as though this was the first we had seen each other that morning. I wondered briefly if he had been aware of our cuddling, or if it had been an instinct. Had he initiated it? Had he wanted it?

He was straight back into professional mode, just like that. And had already pulled out his laptop and was frowning at the screen.

"Are you ready to head down?" He glanced at his watch. "The conference starts soon."

"Uh…" My stomach grumbled. "I could do with something to eat first. And can we get the room sorted?"

"I didn't snore that loud, did I?" He grinned in my direction, and I averted my eyes. I swallowed and tried to compose myself. I couldn't acknowledge him without my mind flicking back to us in bed together, and it wasn't helping my cause to keep myself composed.

"Can we get some room service before we go out?" I changed the subject quickly. "I don't want to go down there on an empty stomach."

"Sure," he shrugged, but he looked a little annoyed. I guessed you didn't get as far as he did in this world by stopping to bother with stuff as pointless as food. I grabbed a menu and quickly called down to order myself a tomato dosa and some fruit juice. They arrived a few minutes later and I ate quickly, feeling Rajesh's impatience. Any kind of intimacy that I thought we'd built up by sharing a bed seemed to have vanished, and now the far more familiar Rajesh was back.

"So, what do you want to cover today?" I asked. I had done my research into the businesses that would be displaying at the conference, but I had no idea which one in particular Rajesh had his eye on. He glanced up at me, and for a split-second it was as though he'd been caught off-guard – like he had been about to tell me the truth.

"I say we just go down and get a feel of the conference today," he suggested. "Maybe we could split up and see if there's anything interesting going on."

"I think it would be better if we stuck together," I replied firmly. I knew that he would take any chance he could to get out from under my feet, to chase down whatever it was he'd come here to do, but he was crazy if he thought he was going to get away from me that easily.

"Fine," he shot back, his voice terse. "I want to talk to Pritath Industries Ltd. and Apollo Technologies specifically. I've heard that the CEO of Apollo has some personal stuff going on right now, might make for a good lead-in to a story to have a human angle."

"Whatever you say," I nodded, and finished up my food, dabbing my mouth with the cloth napkin that came with it. "Shall we?"

"About time," he muttered, and I decided to ignore it. There was no point trying to get him to be more polite with me, when I had bigger things to give a crap about. I grabbed my Dictaphone, a notepad, and a pencil, and followed him out to the lift.

We stood in the lift and I realized that he had his eyes closed. I frowned at him.

"What's wrong?" I demanded, and he glanced over at me as though he'd been pulled from a dream.

"Just getting myself ready," he replied, and he sounded a little embarrassed. I raised my eyebrows. I had assumed that someone who had been in the business as long as he had wouldn't need to psyche himself up to walk into a conference like this. There was something almost comforting about seeing him this vulnerable, and I wondered if he would have shown this side of himself to the woman who had meant to come in my place.

We paused outside the room the conference was taking place in; I could hear the buzz of voices within, the ambience, the excitement. My heart skipped a beat. My first real assignment and I was here with one of the best journalists in the country. It was beyond exciting. Rajesh glanced over at me.

"Are you sure you're ready for this?" He asked.

"It's a little late to replace me, if that's what you were thinking," I pointed out. The whisper of a smile curled on to his lips.

"Fair point," he admitted. "Come on, let's get in there."

We stepped through the doors, and I was hit by a wall of activity that took me a few seconds to adjust to. Like I had expected, there were dozens of stalls and booths from various smaller companies who had come to display their wares in the hopes of getting picked up by a business that could launch them into the fame and fortune they desired – they made up most of the people in the room. But on top of that, there were people making their way around the room slowly, walking with purpose and the self-assuredness of those who knew they were the most important people in a five-mile radius. They had a presence to them that let me know these were the big guys, the guys that everyone here had come to impress – the CEOs and heads of companies like Pritath Industries Ltd. and Apollo Technologies, the ones who had come here to break the next big invention and throw their weight behind the latest tech phenomenon that would take the world by storm within the next few years. I smiled to myself proudly. My research had paid off. I still felt a little out of place, but I knew enough that I could bluff my way through without seeming too much like an amateur.

"We need to pick up our press passes," I reminded Rajesh as we got a hard look from the woman behind a desk near the door. He glanced over at her and then back at me.

"I think we can do without for just a little bit longer," he cocked an eyebrow at me and I furrowed my brow.

"But don't we need it? To be allowed in here?" I pointed out, looking back at the woman – she had been distracted in sorting out some new incomers with passes, and had taken her attention off us. Rajesh took my elbow and steered me into the crowd before she could look back.

"Trust me, it's better for us if we can get in without press passes," he told me, and I pulled my elbow from his grasp. It wasn't that I didn't want him touching me, but that I wasn't sure it would do any good at getting rid of my crush on him.

"Why?" I asked. It didn't make sense. We could get kicked out if they found us in here without the proper identification.

"You'd be surprised at how much those things put people off," he explained as we vanished into the crowd. "People are much more willing to talk to you when they don't know that you might be reporting it somewhere."

"Isn't that a kind of…lying?" I spoke quietly, lowering my voice so no one else could hear me.

"A little," he flashed a smile. "But trust me, we'll get more out of them that way."

"Whatever you say," I held my hands up. "I just want it on record that I tried to change your mind."

"I'll make a note of it." He assured me, and we headed over to one of those suited men who was making their way between the booths. He took up a similar pace and followed close behind.

"What are we doing?" I asked, leaning in to him, and I noticed his eyes were sparkling with excitement. This was what he was good at. This was his comfort zone. I felt myself relaxing and let him take the lead, and dove head-first into my first real day reporting with him.

It went faster than I expected. Frankly, I had been prepared for two straight weeks of dry-as-dust business talk as I tried to find a way to make any of it sound even remotely interesting, but with Rajesh, people seemed a little more inclined to open up about things beyond what was happening at their companies. Rajesh would spot a CEO he wanted to talk to, and make sure he found some way to be idly eyeing the same booth as their assistant. He would get talking, charm them, and the assistant would introduce them to the CEO when they came by, and soon enough, Rajesh would have these powerful characters sharing jokes, anecdotes, and gossip about everyone else at the conference. It was a joy to behold, and I was taking internal notes on how to mimic his skills in getting people to talk to him. He framed me as his assistant, and I scribbled a few surreptitious notes here and there to make sure we remembered the key details of what was being shared with us.

We finished up the day having picked out at least a few major points to follow up on – we had spoken with one of the assistants for one of the partners from Tally, one of the big tech companies native to Mumbai, and she seemed to be pretty certain that they were closing in on a new deal with an up-and-coming company pioneering a new kind of mobile phone, which seemed like a good place to start a story for me. But Rajesh seemed distracted, as though something else was on his mind, as we left the conference after a long day on our feet.

I let out an enormous yawn and covered my mouth to stop from seeming too informal as we made our way out of the conference. But before we escaped, a woman approached us, striding up to us with a certainty that told me she wasn't going to let us get away that easy.

"Excuse me," she announced crossly as soon as she was standing in front of us. "You're Rajesh, aren't you?"

"That's right," he flashed her one of his devastating smiles, but she remained unmoved. Instead, she thrust a couple of lanyards at us, each one holding a small laminated square with "PRESS" printed on it in large letters.

"You'll need to wear these if you want to get back in tomorrow," she warned, and Rajesh slapped the heel of his hand to his forehead as though he couldn't believe he'd forgotten.

"My mistake," he cocked his head at her and pulled an apologetic expression. "Thank you so much for reminding us."

"No problem," she softened for a moment, glancing between us and lingering. "Just don't let it happen again, alright?"

"We won't," I promised and she nodded, satisfied, as we headed out into the hotel lobby. I hooked the lanyard over my neck, but Rajesh shook his head and crammed his into his pocket.

"Keep that off," he ordered. "We're only going to use it to get in and that's it. Alright?"

"Alright," I eyed him curiously. "Am I going to find out why you're acting so secretive?"

"I'm not," He protested. "This is all normal. Ask Priya if you don't believe me."

I cocked an eyebrow at him, not sure whether or not he was serious or if he was just calling my bluff. So I reached into my pocket and pulled out my phone, scrolling through the names until I came to Priya. Rajesh paled at once, and I knew I'd succeeded in rattling him.

"Don't call her," he grabbed the phone off me, and sounded defeated. I looked up at him with a triumphant grin.

"There's something going on here, isn't there?" I leaned in interestedly. "You're here for something you haven't told Priya about."

"Yes," he bowed his head, admitting the truth to me at least. "I am."

"So are you going to tell me what it is?" I demanded, lowering my voice and glancing around to make sure no one was paying attention to us. Rajesh lifted his head and looked back at me, and I could tell he was weighing the pros and the cons of coming out with the truth right there and then. I waited patiently for him to make his mind up, knowing that no matter what he said, I would get the truth out. I would stick to him like glue, and I'd figure it out, even if he didn't tell me. And he seemed to realize that.

"There are these two companies," he leaned in and spoke quickly and quietly. "Pritath Industries Ltd. and Apollo Technologies. They're both here over the next two weeks, and I'm almost certain they're using this conference as a cover to meet and finalise a deal between them."

"So?" I raised my eyebrows. "Businesses working together. That's not against the law, is it?"

"No, but they've always framed themselves as rivals," Rajesh explained. "And I think that they're doing this to try and get control of the industry once and for all. Basically, I think they're trying to wipe out their competition doing this and I know for a fact that that's at the very least highly unethical."

"So you're trying to catch them in the act?" I widened my eyes. His coming here in the first place finally made a lot more sense. He nodded.

"I don't know how, but I'm going to find a way," he replied firmly, and then looked up at me. "Are you in?"

"You want me to help?" I blurted out, louder than I intended – a couple walking by us glanced over at us, and I smiled sweetly until they'd lost interest once more.

"I could always do with someone backing me up," he nodded. "And when it comes to someone like you, you could be more likely to get into places that I can't."

"What do you mean?" I demanded. "You're the one with the credentials."

"A lot of these guys are susceptible to a beautiful woman," he explained, and I felt myself flush bright red at the descriptor.

I brushed away the flattery and focused back on the task at hand.

"So what do you need me to do?" I asked firmly.

"I need you to catch yourself upon all the researches I've done so far and come prepared for tomorrow," he replied. "Can you manage that?"

"No problem," I promised. My head was spinning – I'd just been let in on a secret investigation, and now I needed to keep that secret from Priya while putting me all into getting Rajesh the story he was certain was waiting for him. I suddenly realized that my stomach was grumbling, and knew I'd be able to handle everything better with a little food inside me.

"Where are you getting dinner?" I asked, stretching my arms over my head and wondering how bad it would be if I were to just step out of the high heels that were making my feet ache gratuitously.

"There's a restaurant somewhere in the hotel," he replied vaguely, and it struck me that this was the second time today that he seemed to have forgotten that eating was something he needed to do. "I can get us a table, if you like?"

"What, for the two of us?" I replied stupidly, and he shot me a look that told me it was as silly as it sounded.

"Yes, for the two of us," he nodded. "We'll have to head across now, though. It won't be long till all the vendors are packing up and we won't get anywhere to sit."

"Lead on," I waved my hand and he headed towards a thin corridor that led off the main lobby and reception area and sure enough, a few moments later, we were standing outside a fantastically luxurious restaurant.

"Come on, let's get in before the whole place is full," Rajesh strode into the restaurant like he owned it, while I followed behind, glancing around almost apologetically at the staff. I had never been anywhere that was even close to as fancy as this before. I felt a little out of place, like I was about to be found out at any minute and tossed into some holding pen for people who didn't belong in restaurants like this one. But instead, we were greeted with a warm smile from a waitress who led us to a small, candle-lit table at the opposite end of the room, secluded away from all the hustle and bustle of the hotel. I sat down in my seat and closed my eyes, glad to have a minute to catch my breath and get the weight off my feet.

"This place goes on company credit, right?" I checked, leaning forward and murmuring to make sure none of the staff heard us. Rajesh laughed, a surprising sound. I wasn't sure I'd made him laugh before that. I felt our knees brush up against each other beneath the table, and I bit my lip to keep the shiver running down my spine from becoming too obvious. Seriously, even in the midst of some crazy investigation, Rajesh still had this hold over me that me couldn't explain or justify. Physically, there was just something about him that… well, if I could put it into words, then I might have been able to get over it, but it still felt curiously formless. Maybe that's what made it so exciting, the fact that it still felt so distant and so promising.

"Yes, you're good," he assured me and glanced down at the menus we'd been handed on our way over, "Which is a perfect excuse to eat far more than we should."

"Agreed," I nodded, and sure enough, the two of us got a selection of pretty much everything that sounded good on the menu – fritters, samosas, bhajis, as much as the table to hold without collapsing out from underneath us. I ate and ate and ate until it felt as though I would have to peel down the waistband of my skirt just to stand up again, and leaned back from the table with a long, satisfied sigh.

"That," I announced, "was all amazing."

"It really was," he agreed. "I'll be back here tomorrow, for sure."

"We'll make The Chronicle bankrupt by the time we leave," I joked, and he cocked an eyebrow.

"Sounds like a challenge," he replied, and got to his feet. "Excuse me for a moment."

He vanished off and left me at that table by myself, sitting contentedly and glancing around as the restaurant began to fill up with the other guests. They all looked so much more glamorous than I did, especially the women, and I patted down a few stray strands of hair and checked my Kajal in my reflection in a spoon to make sure I didn't look too questionable. And then, of course, that's when I saw him.

I lifted my head and laid eyes on a man I had truly thought I would never see again in my life. Akshay was just taking a seat about ten metres from me, wearing a suit that his mother had purchased for him years ago and with a haircut that he must have got since we split since I didn't recognise it. He looked good. Well, as good as he could look. What was he doing here? He unhooked a lanyard from his neck and stuffed it into his pocket, letting me know that he was, in fact, at the conference, but he wasn't connected to any of the companies there. Was he? I suppose he could have landed a new job since the last time I saw him. I was staring, unable to take my eyes off him. It felt as though the ground was shifting out beneath me, the same feeling I'd had when he'd told me he was leaving, but this time it felt even more intense for some reason. I knew I should look away, knew I need not torture myself with staring like this, but it was so damn difficult.

The table was half obscured by a pillar that was strategically placed in front of one of the chairs, so when Akshay looked up to see his dinner companion approaching, I couldn't make out who it was. I felt my heart lurch. Who was he taking out to dinner that had his face lighting up like that? Who drew that enormous smile out of him? Who made him get to his feet to lean across and greet them with a… with a kiss?

My jaw dropped as he leaned over to peck whoever it was on the cheek – the pillar was still in the way, but I could tell now that it was a woman; thanks to the glimpse of her shoes and her hands as she dumped her handbag on the ground next to them. He leaned across to take her hands, winding his fingers around them, and I thought about all the times I had tried to show him affection like that in public and all the times he'd knocked me back because he didn't want to make everyone around us uncomfortable. But the way he touched this woman, the way he leaned over to brush her hair from her face – he didn't care who saw him. It seemed like he wanted people to take notice, to be aware that they were together and in love. I felt my heart slip to my shoes as I considered what that said about me. Was this woman, who he could only have been dating for a matter of weeks, really more important to him than I had been?

Suddenly, Rajesh had returned to the table, and my attention was dragged back on to him. He smiled at me curiously, scanning my face.

"What happened?" he asked, sensing that something was amiss right away. "What's going on?"

"Nothing," I shook my head. "I should be getting back up to the room to catch up on all your research. Can you sort the bill?"

"No problem," he nodded. "Are you alright?"

"I'm fine," I assured him, checking to make sure that I had everything I needed before I got out of there. I felt as though the world was crashing in around me, like the walls were closing in, a ringing in my ears making me dizzy and light on my feet. I checked in my pocket for the hotel key, ducked my head down so Akshay wouldn't see me, and headed back up the stairs to our room.

As soon as I was back, I flopped down on the bed and covered my face with my hands. I knew I shouldn't have let it get to me. We were split up, and he was allowed to do anything he wanted. And that included, apparently, taking mystery women out to dinner to the kinds of places that he would have brushed off as far too expensive when the two of us were still with each other. He'd have taken one look at the prices of a place like that, snorted, and suggested we just go back to his family's house and let his mother cook for us. And I could go along with it, because I truly didn't know any better, and that the best way to keep the peace was to let him tell me what to do. I buried my face into my pillow, opened my mouth, and let out a scream muffled by the fabric. I knew I was acting like a teenager, but I felt like I'd been kicked in the stomach, everything I'd been so sure I knew about, my ex-fiancé shifted out from underneath me, making me wonder if all along I had been the problem.

I wasn't sure how long I was lying there, but eventually the door opened and Rajesh made his way into the room. I sat up quickly, smoothing my hair down and hoping he couldn't see the little red rims around my eyes where I'd angrily dashed away some tears at what I'd seen back in the restaurant.

"Are you alright?" he asked, raising his eyebrows at me and taking a step closer to get a better look. I turned my face away from him, not wanting to have this conversation with him. It wasn't like he would give a damn, anyway – he didn't strike me much as the kind of guy who would care much about anything other than the story he was chasing down at any given moment. He never seemed very good with human emotion that he couldn't fit into an editorial.

"I'm fine," I assured him. "Can you forward me all the researches you said you'd done? I need to catch up on that if I'm going to be any help tomorrow."

"Sure," he agreed, and then paused for a moment, eyeing me.

"You're not going to tell Priya about this, are you?" He confirmed, and I rolled my eyes, letting out a little parcel of my frustration on him.

"Rajesh, it's too late for that now," I pointed out. "You don't think I would have already told her if I was going to?"

"Fair point," he conceded and headed for the door. Just before he left, he glanced back over his shoulder.

"Oh, I almost forgot," he remarked, reaching into his pocket and pulling out another key card. "I got us another room."

"Oh, I'll get my stuff-"

"No, it's okay," he cut me off. "I'll go. You stay here and get some rest."

"Thanks," I murmured in his direction as he closed the door behind him, glad that I didn't have to go anywhere. All I wanted to do was curl up in bed, take off my heels, and feel sorry for myself. But before I had a chance to as much as hang up my jacket and crawl back under the covers, there was another knock at my door. I opened it, and found Rajesh standing there with a pile of papers so big that he could rest his chin on them.

"This is all the researches I've done so far," he explained, carefully manoeuvring the papers into my arms. I tried to get a grip on them, but they instantly careened to the right and I had to hurry back to the bed to put them down before they collapsed out of my arms.

"There's... there's so much," I shook my head, eyeing the stack. "How long have you been working on this thing?"

"A long time," he admitted. "About three months, all under the radar – so not a word of this to anyone or this whole thing goes up in smoke, you understand?"

"Of course I do," I nodded. "Hey, if I'm putting myself on the line for you here, I'm getting some credit for this, right?"

"Depends if you sell me out or not," he shot back with a grin, but it wasn't the answer I was looking for. I was edgy and frustrated from what I'd just seen down in the restaurant, and the last thing I needed was for Rajesh to start fooling me around as well.

"Seriously," I gazed at him, imploring him to be honest with me. "You're not going to cut me out of this? Or throw me under the bus?"

"No, I'm not," he met my gaze steadily, unblinkingly. "If you trust me, I trust you. That's how this works."

"You promise?" I asked.

"I promise," he nodded, and I could tell from the tone of his voice and the unwavering way he looked at me that he was telling the truth, that this wasn't a lie. He had done a lot of sneaking around behind people's backs in the last few months, and I supposed a part of him must have been relieved to have everything out on the table like this.

"Why did you tell me the truth?" I blurted out, before I had a chance to think about how the words might sound to him. He leaned against the doorframe and sighed.

"Because you can help me," He shrugged, simply. "I could use someone on my side with this. I've spent so long working without anyone else… I guess I could use an outside influence. Do me good."

"Right," I nodded, feeling cowed. I had wanted him to tell me that it was because I was different, that he knew there was something to me that he didn't see in anyone else we had worked with. I wanted someone to confirm to me that I, for once, was actually special, just in the way that Akshay had proved I wasn't just by being with that new woman. But of course, it was something more pragmatic than that. Of course it was. He barely knew me.

"I should be getting upstairs," he remarked. "I'll catch you tomorrow, first thing?"

"Just knock on my door," I agreed, and watched as he left, shutting the door tight behind him and leaving me all alone. I sat down on the edge of the bed, and eyed the pile of papers sitting on the desk in front of me. At least I had something to keep me distracted tonight. I sighed and reached for the pile, pulling them onto my lap and turning the first page the right way up. Time to get started.

I woke the next morning and turned to the side of the double bed and Rajesh and I had slept on the night before. Sighing, I reached out and placed my hand on the pillow he'd used, longing for the weight of his body in the bed next to mine. I wasn't even sure if it was him that I wanted specifically, or if it was just some kind of comfort, someone to pull me away from the awful thoughts that had been rattling around my head since I had seen Akshay the night before.

I sighed and stood up; heading through for a shower and getting myself dressed and ready to go quickly. I didn't want to sit around in this room any longer. I had spent a good few hours the night before, despite how exhausted I was, reading through all the papers that Rajesh had left me and catching up on the evidences he had that there was something nefarious going on. Even despite how positive he was that all this was going on, I couldn't help but harbour these doubts that this was nothing more than a hare-brained scheme that was going to get the both of us fired. But the evidences he'd acquired were pretty damn convincing. Pritath Technologies Ltd. and

Apollo had been set against each other for years upon years, but someone in the company had given Rajesh a tip-off that something was rumbling between them. A new competitor, Wolfe Technologies, had sprung up, and it looked like they were colluding in an attempt to undermine them and get them taken down. They were planning a deal that would all but render one of Wolfe Technologies' advertisers completely unnecessary. It will destabilise Wolfe Technologies, if the deal went through, and pretty much bring them down. It wasn't necessarily illegal, but it would land them in trouble with a variety of ethics boards and the fact that they were hiding it underlined the fact that they knew. It meant that Rajesh would have to keep it on the down-low, and if someone found out about it, those companies had been known to get rid of the people investigating them. It wouldn't end well for Rajesh if someone was to find out what he was really doing here.

I looked at myself in the mirror – I wasn't sure what it felt like to be on the trail of a story as big as this one, but my palms felt sweaty and my brain was rushing with ideas and thoughts about everything I'd read the night before. I still had a lot of his research to get through – so much of it came in the form of scribbled notes, unfinished email chains and printed-out text messages – but I at least had a grasp on what we were actually looking into and right now that's all I needed to get through the day.

There was a knock at the door and I hurried to answer it. Rajesh was standing on the other side, and he brushed by me and into the room. As soon as our shoulders touched, I felt this little jolt of excitement, and was reminded with no further ado that there was still something about this man that made me more excited than any story could.

"So, I was thinking last night," he turned to me, and his eyes lit up with excitement. I wondered if he'd actually gotten any sleep the night before at all. I had a feeling this was how he came up with a lot of his stories, spending weeks at a time practically climbing the walls as he tried to get the perfect angle, the perfect slice of evidence, the perfect interviewee. Is that what it took to get anywhere in this business? I wasn't sure I had that kind of commitment. But, standing there in front of him as his energy rubbed off on me, I couldn't help but be drawn into his excitement at what was to come.

"I want us to pose as a couple," he suggested bluntly, and my eyes widened.

"What for?" I asked, not wanting to seem too keen, but after what had happened the night before, the thought of actually having someone to be seen with was tempting. Not to mention the fact that it would be Rajesh. The thought of his hand in mine, even just for show, was enough to light embers in my stomach.

"I think people will pay less attention to us if they think we're together," he pointed out. "If it's the two of us as colleagues then people start to ask questions, especially since it's just the two of us. But if we can convince people that I'm just dragging you here while we meant to be on a holiday as a couple..."

"Then they're not going to look into where we're actually from," I nodded. "Sounds like a good idea."

"Plus, I spotted a few pissed-off spouses around the conference yesterday," he cocked his head. "If you could play into that a little bit, you might be able to get them on side and have them tell you something they might not have told me."

"So, we're going to hide who we really are?" I asked bluntly. "Won't that land us in trouble if anyone finds out?"

"We're not going to lie," he shrugged. "We're just… not going to be the ones to bring up who we actually are. There's a lot of ego walking around that conference room and I don't think many of them care much about anyone other than themselves. You'd be surprised at how few of them will actually bother to ask at all."

"I'm in," I nodded, taking a deep breath to ready myself for what was to come. "Oh, I read your research last night, by the way. It's solid stuff."

"I'm glad to hear that," he ran his fingers through his hair, looking at himself in the mirror next to the door. "Sometimes when I get really deep in on a story, I have a hard time actually seeing whether I'm making any sense or not."

I stared at him for a moment as he fixed his hair, not replying; there was something so oddly intimate about seeing him like this, hearing his ideas first-hand instead of through his research, almost like we really were a married couple. I supposed that would help with the con we were about to pull off. I tugged down my skirt and made sure that I looked respectable; what did a married woman look like, anyway? I felt a little pang of sadness when I remembered that only a few months ago I had been sure that I would find out first-hand, but I pushed it from my hand at once. A brief shadow must have passed across my face at the thought, however, because Rajesh briefly frowned at me in the mirror.

"Is everything alright?" He turned to me and peered at me, as though the secret to what I was hiding was literally written on my face. "You've seemed in an... odd mood since last night."

"I'm just tired," I lied, even though part of me wanted to sit down on the bed, burst into tears, and tell him what I'd seen the night before. But I'd only just got him to take me seriously, and that was only going to undermine his new attitude towards me.

"Alright, then let's get going," he suggested.

"Do I look okay?" I asked, brushing my hair back from my face and hurrying to catch up with him. He paused, turned, and looked me slowly up and down. I felt myself flushing at coming under such scrutiny from him. His eyes travelled back up to my face, and he nodded.

"You look good," he assured me.

"Like I could pass for marriage?"

"Like someone would want to marry you," he replied, and I felt my heart skip a beat. How did he still have this much power over me? How was I still so in thrall to every little compliment he threw in my direction? I stepped into the elevator with him and gripped the lanyard in my pocket, letting the laminated corners dig into my palm to distract myself from everything I was thinking about Rajesh and what we could do to each other in the privacy of this lift before the doors opened downstairs.

"Are you okay?" Rajesh asked, pulling me from my little reverie. "You're blushing."

"Uh, it's just warm in here," I tried to cover up the dirty thoughts that had been passing through my mind. "I'm good."

"Good," he nodded. "Got your lanyard?"

"I thought you said we should try and go without them," I replied, confused. "But yeah, I've got it."

"We'll need to use them to get in," he reasoned. "But there's nothing to stop us losing them once we're inside."

"So no one can ask us for them?" I asked.

"That's right," he nodded. "Most of the time, once we're in, no one is going to bother asking for identification. This is the kind of place that everyone feels like they should already know everyone and admitting that you don't is a bad thing."

"So you're going to exploit their egos?" I grinned at him as the doors pinged open and let us out.

"That's our best bet to get this story," he grinned back, and we headed in the direction of the conference hall.

It was packed in there once we got inside, maybe even more than it had been the day before. Everyone seemed a little more hard-edged, maybe that was because we seemed like competition to them now, instead of just bystanders. The vendors seemed more aggressive and the CEOs and partners and managers seemed to have made their minds up about who they were going to go with, and now everyone was in the first stages of threshing out deals that could change the courses of their careers. Of course tension was high. I took a deep breath, and plunged head-first into the mix.

I had never felt the kind of exhilaration I felt that day, not once before in my life. It felt as though my entire body was vibrating with purpose – not to mention the closeness and presence of Rajesh standing right next to me, the occasional casual hand on the small of my back, the light touch to the inside of my arm to get my attention. He was playing the game perfectly, so well that a couple of times I found myself forgetting that we weren't actually here as a real couple. Well, if it was fooling me, then I could be damn sure it was keeping the rest of the conference just as scattered and confused.

Rajesh played it casual at first, strolling around and taking time to stop and talk to a few vendors so it wouldn't look too obvious when we made a beeline for Pritath Industries Ltd. and Apollo Technologies. He was so utterly charming with them that I was almost disappointed on their behalves that he wasn't actually a real business person, but it was clear that he'd pulled this kind of con before. He moved easily around the room, commanding attention but not too much of it. He was perfect, completely in control, and I couldn't help but feel pretty damn lucky that I had landed with him to show me around my first real assignment on the job. I couldn't think of anyone who could have taught me more, or anyone who would have provided better eye candy in the process.

I found myself scanning the room at every opportunity for Akshay. I didn't see him anywhere at any point, but that didn't make me feel any less on edge. In fact, if anything, I felt more so, because if he wasn't here, then what was he doing at the hotel? Had he just swept this new mystery woman away on a romantic trip for two? He had never done anything that spontaneous with me, never even hinted at that kind of lifestyle, and with every passing moment that I considered what I saw of his mystery woman the night before, I felt more and more beaten down. Why hadn't I been worth it? He hadn't shown me even half of the attention and effort he'd shown her in just the tiny glimpses I'd gotten of the two of them together, and it felt pretty terrible to admit that to myself.

"What's wrong?" Rajesh asked as we stood in the centre of the conference hall surveying all that was around us.

"What?" My head snapped up, pulled from the thoughts of Akshay. "Nothing. I'm fine. Sorry."

"Okay," he furrowed his brow at me, clearly not believing my weak protestations. "I see the head of Pritath over there; he looks like he's split away from the rest of the group. Let's see if we can get him talking, huh?"

"Right," I agreed, and he slipped his hand into mine and led me across the hall towards a man I recognised from the research I'd flicked through the night before. As I recalled it, he was named Gaurav, but I couldn't recall his surname. Either way, I plastered a big smile on my face as we approached, and I could have sworn that Rajesh squeezed my hand as we got near. I wasn't sure if that was to reassure him or myself, but I appreciated it, and found myself tentatively squeezing right back. I couldn't believe we were just walking around like this, hand in hand. Every time our bare skin touched, it felt as though it was coming fresh from a dream, my head spinning slightly and my feet feeling as though they were barely scraping along the ground. Suddenly, we were standing next to Gaurav, both of us pretending to pay attention to the spiel that the vendor owner was offering us at hyper-speed, like he knew who he was talking to and didn't want to let him get away.

"….and the processor is going to be faster than anything else in the market, once we get the funding," he continued breathlessly, looking directly at Gaurav who seemed to only be listening to him talk out of a sense of politeness. Rajesh and I exchanged a glance, and I suddenly noticed there was a woman with Gaurav; she was standing a few inches behind him, at his elbow, having been obscured from our sight, thanks to the angle we approached at. I felt my heart skip up and down in my chest. This was my chance. We needed to get talking to them, and she looked as bored by the spiel as I felt. I leaned back slightly, making sure to catch her eye, and she glanced up and smiled in my direction.

"Hello," I mouthed at her conspiratorially, and she ducked a little closer so she could hear what I was saying.

"Do you have a make-up wipe I could use?" I asked quietly, as though embarrassed to bother her. I pointed to a non-existent stain on my shirt. "I need to get this off."

"Yes, I think I have one," the woman rooted in her handbag for a moment and then handed me a moist towel. "Here, that should do it."

"Thank you so much," I nodded in her direction, acting relieved. "I didn't want to look like a slob for the rest of the day."

"Oh, you couldn't, even if you tried," Rajesh smoothly entered the conversation, and finally the vendor finished up and Gaurav turned to see who his companion was talking to. Rajesh glanced up at him, and put out his hand.

"Rajesh," he introduced himself, oozing confidence.

"Gaurav Hanwar," the man replied, shaking his hand and squinting at Rajesh for a moment. "Do I know you from somewhere? I feel like we've met before."

"I'm afraid not," Rajesh shook his head. "I just have one of those faces, I suppose."

There was a moment's pause as the man seemed to doubt his answer, staring at Rajesh, and I could practically feel Rajesh holding his breath as he prayed that Gaurav wouldn't place him from any of his header photos over the years. I spoke loudly and quickly, drawing attention at once.

"Thank you so much for this," I held the make-up wipe up between thumb and forefinger. "I can't believe I forgot to bring any of my own. You're a life-saver."

"No problem," the woman replied, looking at me a little funny. I supposed I was acting like she'd just pushed me from out of the way of a moving car, but if it kept the attention of examining Rajesh and his credentials too closely, I would look like any kind of fool I needed to.

"So, what are you guys here for?" Rajesh asked, gesturing between the two of them. "Just visiting, or…?"

"I run a company," Gaurav rolled his shoulders back and announced it as though we should all have swooned to the ground with impression. I thought I caught the flicker of an eye-roll from his companion, but if I did, she just as quickly returned her face to neutral. "I'm here to see what the little guys have to offer. I like to keep my feet on the ground, you know?"

"Of course," Rajesh nodded sincerely, and I was surprised he had managed to restrain himself from laughing straight in this man's face for being so arrogant. "Any you'd recommend trying out?"

"Well, I suppose I have to say my own company first," he smiled broadly, and reached into his pocket to produce a business card. "Pritath Industries Ltd. You've probably heard of us."

"Of course," Rajesh acted impressed and surprised, exchanging a reverent look with me for show as he plucked the card from between the man's fingers. "I've heard of you. I heard that…"

He trailed off, deliberately leaving the sentence unfinished, and the man leaned forward with interest. "What have you heard?" He pressed, and Rajesh waved his hand as though he didn't want to burden him with what was truly on his mind.

"No, really," Rajesh replied. "It's just a rumour."

"What kind of rumour?" Gaurav demanded, a hard edge appearing on his voice that told us that he wasn't going to back down on this easily.

"Just that you might be making a new deal," Rajesh looked up at the man carefully, as though not wanting to give too much away, and I held my breath. He wasn't really going to announce that he knew what was going on with Apollo this early into the game, was he?

"With Collaborative," he gestured over his shoulder to a small booth about a dozen metres away. I didn't know the name of them, but the booth looked slightly run-down and was certainly not one of the more impressive standings in the room. Rajesh continued, watching the man for a reaction with every word.

"I've been hearing that you're going to work to bring them up," he continued. "I didn't realize how keen the company was on supporting small businesses."

"Where did you hear that?" Gaurav wrinkled his nose up in disgust. "We've got a deal going, but—" He cut himself off before he could say anything more, but Rajesh pounced, sensing an opening.

"Oh, really?" He cocked his head in interest. "With someone big, I bet. I was surprised when I heard people talking about you and Collaborative, since they're so small and you're so..."

He waved his hand up and down, shrugging slightly.

"You know. You're one of the biggest names in the business." Rajesh said.

"You're not reporters, are you?" Gaurav leaned in, and I felt my heart skip a beat in panic. Could we just lie to him? What would happen if we were found out?

"Are we wearing press passes?" Rajesh smiled easily, gesturing between us and pulling me a little closer to sell the whole couple thing once and for all. Gaurav's eyes slid back and forth and he seemed to be considering his options. And then, his ego getting the better of him, he leaned in and lowered his voice.

"Between you and me," he announced, as though he was about to come out with something big, but reconsidered it at the last moment. "We're in a discussion with someone big. You'll hear about it… soon enough."

"Oh, really?" Rajesh raised his eyebrows interestedly. "Who else is involved, if I may ask?"

Gaurav glanced across the room, but then shook his head. "I can't tell you any more than I already have," he lifted a finger to his lips. "I've already said more than I should have."

"Who would we tell?" Rajesh replied with a small laugh, as though the very thought was ridiculous. He was being so careful not to outright lie to this man's face, but at the same time keep the conversation going and stop him pulling back. The man nodded.

"I suppose so," Gaurav agreed. "Anyway, I should be getting away. I have to meet with one of my partners. Enjoy the rest of the conference."

"You too," I replied, and then turned to the woman who was with him. I still wasn't sure if she was his assistant, his wife, his partner, but she had provided us with a way in and for that I wanted to hug her. "Thanks again, by the way."

She waved her hand politely, dismissing my thanks, and the two of them turned to vanish off into the depths of the conference. We waited until they were a reasonable amount of distance away from us, and then Rajesh turned to me.

"That was amazing," he grinned widely at me, his eyes bright and excited, brimming with triumph. "You were amazing. Prisha..."

For a moment, he looked at me, and I found him inching closer, his eyes drifting to my lips, as though he had forgotten himself and was about to kiss me. My breath caught in my throat and my heart began to beat faster, and the sound around us dulled to nothing.

And then the moment vanished when someone at a nearby stall cleared their throat loudly, loudly enough that it caused us to jump back from each other in surprise. I glanced over and found a man regarding us with a cocked eyebrow and a disapproving expression that told me that this wasn't exactly the time or the place to be giving in to how much I wanted this man. Rajesh stepped away from me, the spell broken, and released me from his grasp. After a few seconds, I found the nerve to look up at him once more, not sure where we stood – not sure if that had been part of the act or something far, far more. Because I knew that no matter how deep Rajesh was into the lies he'd constructed, there was no way he could fake something like that. That moment, more than anything else at this conference so far, had been real, deeply and utterly, and I still felt the reverberations of it echoing somewhere deep inside me. Rajesh ran his fingers through his hair and I could tell from the look on his face that it had been as intense for him as it had been for me. In fact, he looked a little taken aback, as though he hadn't expected what we'd shared to have that kind of effect on him.

"I..." he opened his mouth to speak, but a fully-formed sentence seemed to escape him. It was the first time I'd ever seen him speechless, and it was actually a little amusing. I felt a little smirk quirk up on to my face, a complement to the flush that had rushed up my neck and on to my cheeks. My heart was beating fast and my hands already felt as though they were aching to touch him. I knew I should hold back, I knew I shouldn't let this lead anywhere – but I wanted him. I did. There was no denying that any longer, the desire that felt as though it was carried by my blood and pulsing deep into every one of my veins.

"We should get back up to the room," he suggested, and I raised my eyebrows as he quickly corrected himself.

"I mean, we should go note down everything we can remember," he explained. "I just don't want to forget anything."

"That sounds like a good idea," I nodded, and the excitement of the kiss was fading away into something a whole lot more practical and less exciting. I knew I shouldn't have let even that little flush of emotion play on me the way it had, because even if there was something between us – if that moment had been real and not just an attempt to pin down the act – it wasn't like we could act on it anyway. There were still rules in place for a reason, rules that forbade us from doing anything more with each other than we already had. My heart sank. When I found the one guy who made my heart beat faster and my head feel heavy with desire, I couldn't lay a finger on him without getting fired from my dream job.

We turned to head out of the conference hall and we walked in silence, without laying a finger on each other. Had that moment been nothing more than an expression of excitement? I was already over-thinking it and it had been a few minutes since his lips had first met mine. And we still had a few days left together before we could go back to reality and work back at the office. As we stepped into the elevator, I wanted to kick myself for being so stupid as to think that playing a couple with him would end in anything other than a whole host of confusing feelings that I was already struggling to get my head around.

"That was amazing, you know," he remarked, and my head snapped up, eyes wide as I stared at him.

"What?" I demanded, and he seemed to realize exactly how that must have sounded. He swiftly hurried to correct himself.

"The way you got us talking to them," he explained. "I would never have thought of something like that. It was such a smart idea."

"Thanks," I muttered in response. My lips were still tingling from the urge to kiss him, and I touched my fingers to them as though to mimic the feel of his mouth on my own. He seemed to notice, and his gaze lingered on me for a moment before he looked away once more.

"Good job keeping up the act, too," he remarked. I felt my heart drop.

"The couple act?" I asked looking at him.

"Yeah, I think we pulled it off," he nodded.

"Yes, I think we did," I agreed, and felt a little dizziness settle into my head as I tried to make sense of it. "Can I…could you give me a moment? I think I need to take some time to settle into my room. I won't be long."

"Of course," he nodded, gesturing for me to go ahead. "I'll come down to see you in a half-hour?"

"That sounds good, thank you," I nodded. I needed some time away from him, some time to think for myself, because I felt I would lose my mind if I spent another second in his presence. I had no idea what he really wanted from me, if anything, and it was driving me crazy, especially added to my ex-fiancé and his mystery woman the night before. All in all, I was just struggling to get a hold on the men in my life and what they wanted from me and where I stood with them, and it felt like there wasn't enough space in my brain to hold all of that in place right now.

I hurried along to my room as soon as the doors to the lift slid open, not bothering to bid him goodbye. I needed to get out of his presence. It was the only way I was going to make myself feel human again, because when I was around him and the air was thick with the unspoken promise of that kiss, it felt as though I was on another planet.

I fell face-first on to the bed as soon as I was through the door, hoping the darkness and quietness would stop my mind from racing. But, if anything, my head just spun faster than ever before. I had so many questions and no idea how to get answers for them. We'd taken a big step forward with the story, in getting Gaurav to admit that there was a big deal in the works, but I felt like I'd taken a dozen steps back when it came to Rajesh. All those carefully built-up walls I'd put in place to keep myself from getting too attached to him had collapsed around me as soon as our eyes had met on that conference room floor. And I didn't know how I was meant to put them back up again.

"Come on, we need to get something to eat," Rajesh sighed, getting to his feet. We had been sitting in my hotel room for what felt like most of the evening, and my stomach was still churning at being so close to him once more and yet having no explanation or closure about the kiss we'd shared earlier in the day. We'd spent the last hour or so going over what we'd heard from Gaurav and what we needed to find out next to link everything Rajesh had already found out.

"You're right," I agreed, even though my appetite was still stunted. "Restaurant, downstairs?"

"Sure," he shrugged and got to his feet. He had rolled up his sleeves and his hair was a mess from where he'd spent so much time running his fingers through it, but he still looked good – maybe even better than before. I felt as though I was seeing a side to him that no one else did, and there was an intimacy to watching this process unfold in front of me.

We headed to the lift and downstairs, back to the restaurant we'd eaten in the night before. Even though I was still in the clothes I'd been wearing all day and we'd been talking business for the last few hours, I couldn't help but feel a tingle in my stomach at the knowledge that I was about to go out to dinner with a man who I'd shared that heated moment with just a few hours before. It felt like a date.

We managed to grab the last table in the place, as it filled out faster than it had the night before. We slipped into a slightly cramped two-person booth, our knees pressed up against each other beneath the table, and I turned my attention to the menu to keep from staring at him. My heart was fluttering in my chest even as I tried to stem the passion pulsing through my head.

"Oh." A voice next to us drew our attention, and I looked up and saw Lena standing there. She was immaculately put-together, so much so that I shifted in my seat uncomfortably as I became deeply aware of how slapdash I must have seemed in comparison. Rajesh lifted his head with a sense of weary commitment to trying to be civil to her.

"Hello, Lena," he shot me an apologetic look, and she planted her hands on her hips.

"I didn't expect to see you two here," she glanced between us. "The two of you are…together?"

"Yes," Rajesh replied without missing a beat, leaning over and grasping my hand. The shock of his touch, the first time he'd laid a hand on me since that kiss earlier, made my breath catch in my throat.

"Not like you to actually keep someone around for more than five minutes," she eyed me for a moment, something between disdain and pity in her eyes.

"Yeah, well, not every one of my girlfriends hates me as much as you did," he shot back, cocking an eyebrow, and she snorted in amusement, and then looked between us once more.

"She doesn't seem like your type," she remarked, cocking an eyebrow and looking back at him. I bristled with irritation.

"She is also sitting right here," I reminded her, and she glanced down at me.

"I don't buy this," she remarked, and I felt a shiver run up my spine. What would happen if she figured us out?

"You don't have to," Rajesh shot back, squeezing my hand. "Who are you here with, anyway? Or are you having dinner alone?"

"I'm here with someone," she rolled her shoulders back, clearly annoyed. "I can't tell you who. But if you knew…"

She shook her head and grinned to herself, self-satisfied.

"You should probably be getting back to whoever it is," Rajesh suggested. "I'm sure someone that important can't be apart from you for long."

"You're trying to get rid of me," she narrowed her eyes at us. "What are you doing here, Rajesh?"

"I'm writing a story for The Chronicle, I already told you," he replied coolly. "I can't always be running off covering the most interesting stories, you know. I've got to do the groundwork too."

"No, you don't," she shot back. "You get to write about what you want. Why do you want this?"

"Does it really matter?" He remarked, raising his eyebrows. "I mean, why are you here?"

"I'm here because I know there's a good story somewhere and I'm going to find it," she lifted her chin. "And I'm not letting you get to it first."

"Well, good luck," he shot back, and I could feel the energy between them. It might not have been good, but it was there, and it was intense and inescapable and I couldn't help but feel jealous. "You should be getting back to whoever you're here with. I'm sure they're missing your scintillating company by now."

"Good idea," she crossed her arms over her chest. "I guess I'll be seeing you two around."

She peered at both of us again, at our hands touching on the table, and then stalked off, leaving us alone once more. He held on to my hand for another moment before letting go. He shook his head, before craning his neck to see where she had gone to.

"I wonder who she's here with," he muttered, then shook his head "It doesn't matter. She's just saying all that stuff to try and get under my skin."

"It looks like it's working," I remarked, slightly irritated. I knew that they had a history together, but there was something frustrating about the fact that he seemed to be more interested in her than me.

"If she figures out that we're just…" he looked up at me, and I held my breath as I waited for him to finish his sentence. If we were just faking it?

"It doesn't matter," he shook his head and got to his feet to crane his neck. "She doesn't matter. Are there any damn waiters around here?"

I stood up with him, looking around, and noticed that Lena was still eyeing us.

"She really doesn't buy this," I remarked.

I paused for a moment, looking at him, my gaze flicking down for a moment to his lips. His eyes met mine, and just looked at me for a moment. And for a split second, something changed behind his eyes. I wasn't sure what, but it was enough to make my heart sing with the promise of it, to make me want to melt against him and finally give up this pretence of being platonic. He caught my face in his hands, tilting my chin up so I was looking right at him. I blinked back, not sure whether this was part of the act or something more and not caring to make the distinction clear. And then, all at once, he leaned in and kissed me.

His lips were surprisingly soft against mine – that was the first thing that crossed my mind, because I was in such shock that I couldn't process anything else. His hands slipped down my sides to wrap around my waist, and I found myself sliding my arms around him, pulling him close, enjoying the feeling of the strength of him against me like this. He pushed his tongue against mine and soon we were kissing deeply, our bodies in perfect concurrence as I inhaled the sweet scent of his aftershave. His stubble was slightly rough against my chin, but I didn't care. I couldn't have cared about anything at that moment, but how strong his arms felt around me, the sensation of his thumb as it traced a path lightly across my waist. I felt something tingle to life deep inside me, something that had been asleep for a long, long time.

There we were, standing in the middle of that restaurant, completely and utterly and happily lost to each other, like nothing else in the world mattered, and for those blissful few seconds, my brain was beautifully blank and I could forget every single thing in the world apart from how good I felt kissing him. How natural this was. How I could have done this all day and not cared a jot for the people who stared at us. The conference, the article, the web of lies we'd built to get to this point – it didn't matter as long as he had me in his arms, as long as I was his. He pulled back slowly, as though unwilling to break the kiss.

"That should convince her," he remarked, and he shifted forward as though he intended to kiss me once more. In that moment, I knew that if he suggested we leave that place right then and there and took me back to the hotel room upstairs, I wouldn't stop him. But then, he leaned back in his seat and picked up his menu, and the spell was broken. I looked down at my own menu, and glanced over at Lena, who I found looking back at me with distaste. I grinned to myself. Well, if nothing else, at least I had proved to her that the two of us were better than she and him were.

We ate dinner, quietly discussing what we'd found out earlier in the day and trying not to catch anyone's attention. Dinner was good, as it had been the night before, but I felt uneasy for reasons that I couldn't put my finger on. Or perhaps it was just that I didn't want to.

"I want to get an early night," I blurted out once we were finished eating. I could tell he wanted to talk longer, but I needed to get out of there before I said or did something I couldn't take back.

"Of course," he waved his hand. "I'll take care of the bill. You get some rest. It's been a busy day. And I need you in good form for tomorrow. You're turning into the brains behind this operation."

"Just watch me," I responded, a little weakly, and he grinned back. I couldn't believe how much things had changed just over the last few days; he had gone from being so mad at me having to come along on this trip in the first place to the two of us against the world. I guessed that was the power of a secret shared; it bonded us together, left blurred edges around our supposedly platonic relationship. The best thing I could do, if I couldn't cut myself off from him completely to let logic get the better of my heart, was to remind myself of what was on the line if I pursued my true desires.

I headed back upstairs, curling up in bed again, and found myself just as lost as I had been before – maybe even more so, thanks to that kiss. I had no idea what to make of it. I couldn't find the line between truth and fiction any more, and, as a journalist, that line was more important to me than most. I needed to get some sleep, unwind, then go into that conference tomorrow anew and focus on getting this story instead of getting the guy.

As we stood in the lift on the way down to the conference the next day, I couldn't help but notice that things felt different between us. It felt like the memory of the kiss was hanging heavy over our heads, reminding us just how far we were already into this – and just how much we had to lose to be continuing.

"Are you alright?" Rajesh asked again, and I didn't move my eyes from the fixed point I had focused them on as soon as I'd walked into the lift with him. I didn't want to look at him – no, that still felt too dangerous, as though I might give in and throw myself at him like I'd been longing to do since he'd stopped by my room first thing to pick me up. Bright and early, that's what he'd said, but I felt as though I could do with another ten hours of sleep – I had tossed and turned the entire night and I was still exhausted, despite vanishing back upstairs right after dinner.

"I'm fine, honestly," I nodded firmly. I didn't need his scrutiny right now; in fact, even just feeling his eyes on me was enough to get my blood rushing to my face. I shifted my weight from foot to foot, fighting back a yawn.

"So, what do you want to do today?" I asked, and he frowned slightly.

"I was thinking about it last night," he began, slightly hesitant. "I was looking into the events for the conference, and there's a big, fancy party tonight for the CEOs and higher-ups of most of the companies – seems quite renowned for gathering a lot of very important people in one room and getting them really drunk."

"And maybe a little loose-tongued?" I filled in the blanks, and he nodded.

"That's what I'm hoping for," he confirmed. "But we need to get in there first."

"And we're not doing that with a press pass alone, I guess?" I asked him.

"That's right," he nodded. "So we need to find some way to get into that party and see if we can get some more confirmation on my research. I want to have something to give to Priya by the end of the day."

"You're going to tell her?" I widened my eyes at him, panic lancing through my system. "Won't we end up in a lot of trouble?"

"We're going to end up in a lot of trouble either way," he flashed me a smile, as though the very thought of it excited him a little. "But I figured it's better for her to know sooner rather than later. Not to mention, I might be able to use her name to get into this party if she calls ahead."

"Really?" I was surprised.

"Really," he nodded. "She's a big name, maybe big enough that we could get in if she agrees to let us use it."

"I don't see how that works," I shook my head, frowning.

"Her family owns The Chronicle," he reminded me. "It's a business, even if it's not the kind that we see a whole lot here. But she could claim that she's sent some representatives to mingle, maybe to find some new tech partners for the newspaper?"

"So, we'd stop lying to one person to start lying to another bunch of people?" I confirmed, cocking my head at him. He shrugged.

"More or less," he replied, as though it was nothing. "But, don't worry about it. I've got this under control."

"Whatever you say," I sighed. The lift doors opened in front of us and we headed down to the conference.

Same as the day before, we posed as a couple and made our way around trying to find someone to bring us along to the party that evening. We tried to locate Gaurav again, but to no avail, and I found myself getting exhausted and frustrated as we struggled to find somebody who actually seemed like they could be an in for us. But everybody seemed a little more reserved that day, as though they were waiting to unleash the wildness at the party that evening. Most of the big names weren't even on the floor.

"Everyone's holding out for tonight," Rajesh muttered as we made our way through one more loop of the conference hall, only to come across no one who'd be of any significant use to us.

"So what do we do?" I glanced at him, slightly nervous, because I knew what was going to come out of his mouth next.

"We need to call Priya and get her to pull some strings for us," he replied firmly. My shoulders slumped. I knew she was going to find out about this one way or the other, but I had hoped that we could put it off a little longer. Rajesh eyed me for a moment, and he must have been able to sense my hesitation.

"I'll take all the blame for this," he promised. "Don't worry. This was all my idea in the first place and I'm not going to drag you into it with me."

"You sort of already have," I pointed out, feeling my heart rate picking up a little in my chest. I had always been the kind of person who made sure they were always doing the right thing, even when it was tough, and here I was lying to the woman who had hired me for my dream job. Even if it was for a good cause, I still felt uncomfortable.

"I'll make sure Priya puts all the blame on me." He briefly reached down and squeezed my hand, and I jolted slightly at his touch. As soon as our skin connected, any question of asking him not to leaked out of my head at once. Did he know the effect he had on me? Was he just exploiting my attraction to him? I honestly had no idea and it was beginning to unsettle me. Nobody had ever held this much power over me with just a look, and I was scared that he would figure that out and start using it in ways I wasn't sure about – if he hadn't already.

"Come on, let's go get this call over with." He sighed, dropping my hand and sending me crashing back to earth. I followed him out of the conference and back up to his hotel room, my brain racing the entire time. Would I lose my job for this? And if I didn't, should I? I hadn't lied to Priya, but I hadn't told her the whole truth as well, and she had only sent me along on this thing in the first place, because she trusted me to keep an eye on the man she still didn't have a solid grasp on herself. I perched on the edge of the bed, watching as he paced back and forth, slowly rolling up his shirt sleeves and running his hand through his hair over and over again. He didn't say a word to me, but he didn't have to. I knew he was trying to figure out what to say to Priya to keep her on his side.

"We could just try to sneak in to that party tonight," I suggested. "Put off telling Priya a little longer and focus on confirming more of the story—"

"I'm not sure how much longer I can keep this going without her finding out," he shot me a look, and I wasn't sure if he was trying to insinuate that I might tell her, but it put my hackles up nonetheless. Was he testing me?

"She knows this kind of thing isn't the sort of story I usually go after," he reasoned. "She's bound to be wondering why I'm showing such an interest in this now. She'll be doing some research of her own, maybe checking my correspondences over the last few months—"

"You really think she'd do that?" My eyes widened. He shrugged.

"I know I would if I could," he pointed out, and grabbed for his phone. "I knew I'd have to tell her sooner or later. I just hoped we'd have more by now."

"You're going to do it?" I blinked up at him, fear shooting through my body. He nodded.

"I have to." He sighed. "I don't want to, but I need her right now. I need her to get us in."

He dialled a number, put the call on speaker phone, and tossed it down onto the bed before sinking down next to it himself. Despite the panic the situation was arousing in me, I couldn't help but notice that the two of us were alone together once more – just me and him, in this bedroom together – just like we had been on that first night. I shifted nervously and shoved the thought from my head. It wasn't doing me any good right now to linger on to how strong his arms looked as he flexed his fingers back and forth to work off his nervous energy.

"Priya here," Priya's voice, slightly crackly, came across the line and made me jump. Rajesh took a deep breath, and then launched into it.

"Priya, I need your help with something," he began confidently, so confidently that I couldn't believe he was about to put his career on the line in the next few sentences. Was he always this collected and calm? I hoped that one day I'd find that kind of poise.

"Go for it," Priya replied, and I could hear a hint of suspicion in her voice. She must have had some idea of what this was about. Rajesh looked up at me, as though giving himself one more push to actually get the words out, and then launched into it.

He told her everything – every detail of the story he'd researched so far, plus everything we'd picked up after a couple of days at the conference. She didn't react – at least, not verbally – and somehow her silence was a whole lot worse than anything she could have come out and said. I sat stiffly next to Rajesh, hands folded in my lap, and realized after a minute or so that I hadn't taken a breath. I inhaled sharply and deeply, filling my lungs with air, and Rajesh shot a look up at me – he reached over to touch my leg, just lightly, a gesture meant to calm me, but that instead sent a shock of desire across my skin. Well, it was enough to distract me, at least.

"...so we need you to call ahead and see if you can get us in," he finished up at last. There was a long, long silence, and after what felt like an age, she spoke again.

"So you're telling me that you researched this by yourself, without clearing it with me, and then took off across the country on The Chronicle's dime to try and find out if any of this was actually true?" She confirmed.

"That's right," Rajesh agreed. It sounded bad when she put it like that, but I was confident that Rajesh had a good reason for doing what he'd done. Or maybe I'd just spent a little too long around him and his all-too-convincing ego? I couldn't be sure anymore.

"And you expect me to just step in and help with that? After you have lied to me?" She snapped. Rajesh opened his mouth to continue, but, as if sensing it, Priya stormed on, her voice dripping with disdain and distrust.

"You have to understand how this looks to me, Rajesh," she continued. "You lied to me, and the company, and you're only telling me the truth now because you need me to help you out. How long would it have been if you hadn't needed my help? Would I have ever found out?"

"Of course you would," he assured her, but he pulled a face at me that indicated that he wasn't sure how true that actually was.

"Is Prisha with you?" She asked, and I opened my mouth but found that nothing was coming out. Rajesh touched my waist, jolting me back into reality.

"Y...yes, I'm here," I spoke louder than I had to, as though worried that she might not hear me somehow.

"And you knew about all of this?" She confirmed. I nodded, and then remembered that she couldn't see me.

"I did," I admitted, and she let out a long sigh, a crackle of static running down the line.

"You should have come to me," she admonished me. "You know that I wouldn't have allowed this. Why did you think this was the right thing to do?"

"I…I…" I trailed off, looking at Rajesh and finding myself briefly lost in his eyes. I knew the answer to that question – it was because I didn't know how to say no to him. Even if I'd wanted to, even if I could have dug down and found some way to remind myself that I should have told Priya all of this first, I couldn't have done it, because all I wanted in the world was for him to like me and want me and need me. But I couldn't say any of that to Priya – not without landing in more trouble than I already was in so I swallowed what I truly wanted to say and tried to fill in the blanks as best I could.

"I don't know," I sighed, and shot him a dirty look, even though I knew this was as much my fault as it was his. "I'm sorry."

"You should be," she replied briskly, as though it should have been obvious. "You're both in a hell lot of trouble for this."

Rajesh held his breath, glancing over at me.

"I'll get you into that party tonight." She sighed.

"Thank you, Priya," Rajesh punched the air in excitement, but she wasn't finished speaking yet.

"But if you can't come up with a story, then you'll both be fired."

The words hung in the air between us, the entire world grinding to a halt around us as we took them in. I sucked in a sharp breath; the stakes had suddenly launched into the catastrophic for me. Rajesh and I exchanged a glance, one that was full of horror at what we'd just heard, as though checking in that yes, for real, that was what Priya had just said to us. Rajesh took a deep breath, closed his eyes, and continued talking, this time faster than before, as though it was even more important that he got the words out.

"I take full responsibility," he hurried. "Prisha had nothing to do with the planning of this; she just went along—"

"Yes, she went along," Priya cut him off. "I'm not interested in hearing any of your excuses, Rajesh. Just know that this is what you're facing up to with this. Are we clear?"

"We're clear," Rajesh nodded, apparently coming to terms with the fact that she wasn't going to change her mind. My head was spinning. If I'd known all this was on the line, would I have gone along with it? I had no idea. Probably. Maybe. It was just so exciting to be swept along on something like this that I wasn't sure I had it in me to stop it short.

"Good," Priya sounded grimly satisfied. "I'll message you once I've got everything sorted for the party."

"Thanks again," Rajesh managed, and then she hung up. He closed his eyes and flopped back on to the bed, throwing his arms out wide as though trying to embrace the enormity of the situation. I stared off into space, already wondering how I could possibly tell my mother – who had been so very proud of everything I'd pulled off with getting this job – how I ended up fired in less than a month. She would kill me for this. Heck, I would kill me for this, if it ended up getting me canned.

"I'm so sorry," Rajesh sat up, sliding a hand up my back and placing it on my shoulder. For a second, any panic about what we'd gotten ourselves into vanished as all I could think about was the sweetness and softness of his touch, of how close his fingers were to lightly caressing my neck.

"No, I didn't have to get involved." I sighed. "It's my fault as well, just like Priya said."

"It's not," he replied firmly. "And I'm going to do everything I can to make sure that you don't take any flack for this, okay?"

"Whatever you say," I replied, my voice weary even to my own ears.

"Okay," he got to his feet, pulling his hand from my shoulder. The absence of it felt oddly empty, and I fought the urge to grab his hand, to pull him back down onto the bed with me.

"We've got to make the most of what time we've got here," he announced. "We have to make this count. So let's get our game faces on for the party tonight and come up with a plan."

"O...okay," I managed, nodding along with him. I had no idea what I was meant to do from here on, but I knew it had to be good if I wanted to keep my job. I straightened my back, set my face in neutral expression, and tried to put myself into the mindset that I would need to be in if we were going to make this work. Now it was more than just a great story – our jobs were on the line too. And I was going to do everything in my power to make sure that I kept mine.

I tugged a strand of hair loose from the bun I had pulled the rest of it up into, letting it come down around my jaw to frame my face. For someone who had no idea that they were going to be at a fancy event, I thought I looked pretty good. I had managed to pull together something resembling a party-appropriate outfit out of the wardrobe I had brought with me to the conference. I had started from the bottom up, with a pair of heels that elevated me a few inches so I wouldn't look quite as tiny next to Rajesh. My long, often unruly dark hair was pulled back high on top of my head, and actually pulling it back from my face reminded me that I had cheekbones and a jawline under there. I had outlined my eyes with dark, forest-green liner to pull out the emerald flecks in my woody-brown irises, and I'd even dug up a deep wine-coloured stain to paint my lips with. I usually avoided lip colour as I was a little self-conscious about how big my lips looked with it on, but tonight I enjoyed the way the dark stain drew attention to their fullness. My outfit was simple, but I thought I looked chic enough – a skirt that hugged my hips and flared out a little over my waist, and a figure-hugging top that I usually wore with something over the top of it, but tonight was allowed to fly solo. It was a little low-cut, dipping to reveal a few inches of cleavage in a way my mother would have disapproved of, but I liked the way it made my body look – curvy and playful. I had slipped an anklet over my right ankle, and even headed down to the in-house hotel salon for a manicure, my nails painted a deep purple and shaped perfectly. I pouted at myself in the mirror. Yes, this would do. For a second, I thought of Rajesh behind me, his approving gaze sweeping up and down me as a smile curled on to his mouth.

There was a knock at my door, and I went to open it. Rajesh was standing there, dressed in a slightly crumpled shirt and a dark blue blazer that brought out the flecks of grey in his eyes. As he turned and cast his eye on me for the first time, his mouth opened in surprise.

"What's wrong?" I frowned. "Don't I look right?"

"No, you look..." He trailed off and waved his hand as though the words escaped him. His eyes travelled down over my body, taking in the curve of my waist and traversing down my legs for a moment before he returned his gaze to my eyes.

"You look perfect," he replied, with a studious nod. "We should get going to the party. We don't want to be late."

"Sounds good," I agreed, and he offered me his arm. I stared at it for a moment, not quite registering what he was asking for, until I remembered that we were meant to be posing as a couple together once more. I slipped my arm through his, and tightened my grip, enjoying the strength of his beneath my fingers. He felt good. This felt good; natural, almost. As if this was how we were always meant to be.

I cleared my brain and focused on the task at hand. I had to keep my head in the game if I wanted to get this story and hold on to my job, though doing all that while on the arm of the most handsome man I had ever seen felt like playing the game on hard mode.

We made our way downstairs to the party, and found ourselves standing outside the door to a small, nondescript looking room that I wouldn't have glanced at twice had I just been making my way by. I frowned and tried to peer around the smart-dressed woman at the door, but she calmly moved to block my view.

"How can I help you?" she asked, shooting me a look that told me if I tried to do that again, she would have no problem kicking me out. It was clear that whatever was going on in that wasn't for the eyes of the general public, and that just made me even keener to see behind the door.

"We're here with The Chronicle," Rajesh announced, as though it should have been obvious. And even though Priya had assured us that she had everything in hand, I still felt a little shiver of nervousness as I worried that the woman might laugh us out of there anyway. She ran her hand down the list she had in her hand and nodded once, apparently satisfied.

"You're on the list," she smiled warmly at the both of us, her demeanour changing at once as soon as she realized that we were actually meant to be here. "Please, go ahead."

She stepped aside, and Rajesh and I exchanged a relieved look as we headed past her and into the room beyond.

My jaw dropped as soon as I stepped inside – it was stunning, nothing like the rest of the hotel which looked positively utilitarian in comparison. No, this room was clearly made up to impress. It was cavernous but carefully filled and made-up with stylish soft lighting and dark, polished wood that seemed to shine in the dim light. There was a band playing at the other end of the room, not far from the generously stocked bar, and my eyes travelled over the packed-out floor in front of us; the who's-who of the tech world was mingling, chatting each other up over glasses of champagne and looking as though they were having the time of their lives.

"Okay, where do we start?" Rajesh asked softly, leaning over to me. I caught a whiff of his aftershave, which he had applied liberally, and it filled my senses so much that I felt I might keel over on the spot. It was all so much.

"I think," I began, breathing slowly and deeply and doing my best to keep myself together. "I think we should find someone we need to talk to and wait till they are drunk enough for us to get something out of them."

"And until then?" Rajesh asked, grinning. He was glancing at the bar, and I knew precisely what was going through his head.

"Maybe just one," I agreed, and he led me across the crowded floor to the bar on the other side of the room. The drinks were free, and both of us plucked a glass from the tray that was sitting out on top of the counter. The bartender, a young man, flashed me a very warm smile and I felt myself flush slightly. I wasn't used to having attention paid to me in that way and it still felt a little like a mistake when someone did look at me like that. Rajesh glanced between me and the bartender, and slid his arm around my waist; it could have been a casual gesture, but it felt more possessive, as if he was letting this young man know who I was with. I found myself leaning into him, and noticed that his thumb was tracing lightly up and down my waist. He didn't have to do that. But I certainly wasn't stopping him.

I took a sip of the champagne in my hand, the bubbles fizzing around my head and instantly making me relax. We turned to the floor and began to scan it for whoever we could find.

"There's Gaurav," He nudged me. "Come on, let's see what kind of state he's in."

"Do you think the Apollo Tech people will be here too?" I asked, and he nodded.

"I'd be stunned if they're not," he assured me, and then a big smile broke out across his face. "In fact, there they are, talking to Gaurav, right now."

"Are you serious?" I gasped, and finally my vision focused on the small cluster of people to the right side of the room. Gaurav was there, and he was with two others that I recognised from the research that Rajesh had done. One was Samar Sidana, the other Anaya Luthra – the two partners who ran Apollo Tech. And there they were, in the middle of the room, chatting away to each other like they didn't run two companies who were completely and almost always at loggerheads with one another.

"Should we dive in?" I asked, but Rajesh shook his head.

"Let's see if anyone else has noticed that there's something wrong with that," he leaned in close again, and I could feel his breath against my skin. It was intimate, almost too intimate, considering we were in a room full of people.

"Let's go." He marched out into the floor, all confident, and I let him pull me along beside him. I didn't want to break free of him, didn't want to move from his side for a moment. He made me feel safe, even in the mess that this conference was turning out to be for the two of us.

We dived into conversations, the two of us finding our ways into various discussions with the little groups that were clustered around the room. We weren't the only ones who'd noticed that there was something up with the fact that Apollo Technologies' and Pritath Industries' heads were actually talking to each other. A woman mentioned to us that she'd seen them actively avoiding each other the year before, and another dropped a couple of hints towards the fact that she'd heard of a deal being brokered between them, though she didn't give us any details. Rajesh and I exchanged triumphant looks; news of this deal was beginning to spread, that much was clear. Now, we just needed to hear something from the people themselves on the matter, an admittance that we could use to pin them down on everything that we were already sure was true.

We moved through the crowd towards them, and when we got there, it was clear that the three of them were quite drunk – they were gesturing wildly, laughing loudly, and leaning in and chatting conspiratorially to each other. It was so blindingly obvious that there was something going on; they were being so brazen. But I supposed that when you had been on top of the game for this long it meant that maybe you forgot what it was like to have anything to worry about. Well, maybe we could do something to put them back on their toes and remind them that they weren't infallible.

Suddenly, the woman, Anaya, broke away and headed for the bathroom.

"You go after her," Rajesh nodded in her direction. "See if you can get anything out of her while she's away from the other two."

"Right," I agreed, and waited a little for her to get ahead of me and then went after her. Rajesh smiled at me encouragingly, and then headed over to join the men. I took a deep breath and went after her, walking quickly, my glass of champagne still clamped in my hand. And then, of course, that's when I saw him.

I came to a dead halt, even though I knew he shouldn't have bothered me. Akshay? Again? I was sure I'd seen the last of him in that restaurant, but here he was, dressed in the same suit he'd worn to my graduation and leaning up against the bar. He was looking around casually, as though waiting for someone, and I was frozen to the spot. I knew that if he saw me he could blow this whole thing wide open, and I ducked to keep away from his scanning of the area around him. My heart was beating faster, and I cursed myself internally for still having this intense reaction to his presence. I knew that he was out there, after all. He was staying in the hotel, and why else would he have been here if not for the conference? But the one thing that didn't make sense was how he'd ended up in this party. It seemed pretty exclusive, and while we'd been together, he hadn't been working for any tech companies that I was aware of. This had to be a new job, unless he'd found some way to sneak in here like Rajesh and I had. I kept my head down and continued on my way to the bathroom, taking deep breaths to steady myself.

How could I let him be doing this to me? How could he still affect me this deeply? I ducked into a cubicle, not catching the eyes of any of those women who were primping in the mirror around me. I could barely focus on them anyway. But the problem wasn't that I was just hurt seeing Akshay again. No, it was more than that. My head was spinning because all I wanted right then and there was to go find Rajesh and throw myself into his arms because I knew he would make it better. I knew that's how it would work.

I composed myself and headed back out to the sinks, where the woman I had been sent after was washing up. I took a deep breath and stepped up beside her, offering her a weak smile in the mirror in front of us. She barely even glanced at me, her smile flickering the tiniest amount before she picked up her bag and turned to go.

"Excuse m—"

Before I could get the words out, she was gone, and I was left staring at myself in the mirror. I washed my hands, touched my hand to my hair to fix it back into place, and followed her out. I needed to get back out there and support Rajesh.

I found my way back to his side, and he slipped an arm around my waist as though it belonged there. He was in conversation with Samar and Anaya, but it didn't look like it was going too well.

"So, I was speaking to Gaurav yesterday—" he began, but Samar held his hand up to cut him off.

"We don't need to hear anything about Gaurav," he replied coolly. "He's the last person I want to hear about."

"Oh," Rajesh breezed by the rudeness. "It's just that—"

"Who are you, anyway?" Anaya frowned at him, and then glanced over at me. "And who's she? She was in the bathroom back there…"

"Come on," Rajesh tugged me away from them before they went any further. His brow was furrowed and it was clear that this night hadn't gone as planned. I felt the same way. Akshay's presence having thrown me completely off-guard. He sighed, finishing his drink in one last sip.

"This is a bust," he sighed, and he reached over to pluck a bottle of champagne from a nearby ice bucket. He tucked it under his arm.

"What are you doing?" I widened my eyes at him in shock.

"We're getting out of here," he replied. "The last thing I want is any of them to figure out who we are or what we're doing here."

"And you're taking that champagne?" I couldn't help but grin, despite myself, despite knowing all the trouble that we were probably about to dump ourselves into.

"Well, we're not coming out of here with completely nothing." He flashed me a playful smile, took my hand, and we headed for the door. I couldn't believe what was happening.

"Are we seriously stealing a bottle of champagne?" I hissed as we headed out of the packed-out room, and he glanced back over his shoulder.

"Only the best," he replied, and before I knew it, we were headed in the direction of my hotel room, the honeymoon suite that they had mistakenly given us our first night. I should have found somewhere else to stay, but there was something nagging at the back of my mind that told me that I might need to use it.

He opened the door for me, glanced over his shoulder, and we headed inside together. He still had the bottle of champagne. I couldn't believe he'd thought to do something like that. I had always been so committed to doing the right thing that, had it not been for the terrible night I'd been having so far, I'd have demanded that he take it back down to the party and apologise for pinching their best booze. As it was, I already wanted a glass.

"Bottle opener?" He asked, and I tossed him the one that sat on top of the untouched drinks bar. In one smooth motion, he caught it out of the air and pulled it to the champagne bottle, popping the cork a second later.

"Smooth," I remarked, with a cocked eyebrow. He grabbed one of the glasses that sat on top of the drinks' bar and deftly poured us both a drink.

"Just watch me," he teased in response, handing me the glass. Our fingers touched ever so slightly, just for a moment, and I felt that spark again. Or maybe I was just excited to be getting into some ridiculously expensive champagne. It was certainly one or the other. I took a sip, the bubbles fluttering up my nose. It tasted good.

"Were you alright back there?" Rajesh nodded back in the direction of the room we'd just come from. "You seemed a little…off."

"I just…" I trailed off. Was I really going to tell him this? I knew I should have kept things professional, but I felt like we were long beyond that at this point. Somewhere between stealing the champagne and taking back to a honeymoon suite, professionalism had long since left the building.

"I saw my ex," I replied, throwing my free hand in the air. Rajesh raised his eyebrows, looking taken aback.

"Your ex?" he asked.

"Yes, I have an ex," I cocked my head at him. "Or does that come as a surprise?"

"Certainly not," he replied with a half-grin. "Go on."

"I don't know what the hell he was doing there, but it's the second time that I've seen him at the hotel," I went on, the words pouring out of me. I realized how desperately I'd tried to keep all these feelings down before now, how much I'd needed to let them out.

"How long have you guys been broken up?" Rajesh asked.

"Oh, I don't think there will ever be enough time between Akshay and me," I grinned wryly. "We split up a few months ago, out of nowhere."

"He doesn't seem like much," he shook his head.

"You didn't even see him!" I protested.

"But if I didn't notice him, then he wasn't that much," he replied, and I finally let myself laugh.

"Fair point," I admitted. "I just... I thought I left him behind, but I didn't. Seeing him was still difficult."

"Of course it was," Rajesh shrugged. "He sounds like a jerk, if that makes you feel any better."

"You don't know anything about him," I protested.

"I know that he left you." He pointed out, taking a sip from the glass in his hand.

"Maybe he had a good reason," I threw back.

"Whatever it was," he replied slowly, "I strongly doubt it was good enough."

Our eyes met, and I knew that if he got to his feet right then, came to me, and kissed me again, then I would be jelly in his hands. His words had me melting in his hands. I wondered if this was intentional. I shifted in my seat, breaking the moment, the alcohol rushing around my head. I needed to put a stop to this, and quickly, before things got too far out of my control.

"I should probably be getting some rest," I remarked, running my fingers through my hair and crossing and uncrossing my legs nervously. I was still so dressed-up, and he looked amazing in his suit, and the champagne in my hand and the secrets I was sharing made this whole thing feel a lot more intimate than it had any right to.

"If you want," he replied, and took another sip of his champagne and got to his feet. Before I knew it, I was blurting out something, anything to make him stay.

"What about you?" I asked, staring up at him. He paused and turned to me.

"What about me?" He asked directly looking at me.

"Your ex is here too, right?" I reminded him. "But you don't seem that bothered."

"I was never that bothered about Lena," he snorted. "We were just meant to be a bit of fun, that's all. But she got attached and I guess I was a little harsher than I had to be about calling things off."

"Why, what did you do?" I asked.

"I travelled halfway across the country to chase a story and only told her when I was at the airport," he shrugged, and I spluttered in surprise.

"You did what?" I could not retain my surprise.

"I didn't realize how into the relationship she was till then," he replied, leaning up against the desk that held the enormous TV. "She was furious with me. I guess she still is."

"I can't believe you'd do something like that," I shook my head. "No wonder she hates you."

"Yeah, maybe I'm as bad as your ex," he remarked, meeting my gaze as though daring me to contradict him. I opened and closed my mouth, not sure what to tell him. If I'd been in Lena's position, I'd have been pretty angry with him. But it was different with him. It had to be. Because if it wasn't, then I was just falling for the same crap that Akshay had served up to me for all those months, and I couldn't bear the thought of that.

"I don't think you could be," I raised my eyes to meet his and found that my voice had gone hoarse. I took a sip of champagne to moisten my vocal cords once more, and cleared my throat. Was this room having an effect on me? Because I felt like I was being haunted by the randy memories of past honeymooning couples, and I was looking at Rajesh with pretty much unbridled desire at that moment, willing to make excuses for anything he told me because I felt the urge to be with him that badly. The way he was looking back at me told me that he was feeling much the same way. Despite the failure of the night so far, we could salvage it. We could make it special. We could turn it around.

He looked away from me, finished up his glass of champagne, and headed for the door without a second glance. The suddenness of his movements took me by surprise, and I found myself on my feet, fighting the urge to follow after him – or to beg him to stay with me for the night, to hold me like he had that first evening we'd spent together in this place.

"I should get out of here," he muttered. "We've got so much work to get done tomorrow. I don't want to be hung-over."

"Yes, of course," I gestured for him to go, forcing myself to look away. I knew if I met his gaze one more time, then I wouldn't be able to get rid of him.

"See you tomorrow," he replied, carefully replacing the glass on the counter and closing the door behind him. As soon as he was gone, I leaned up against the solid wood between us, closed my eyes, and tried to get my head straight. I wanted to be with him so badly, but everything that surrounded us was telling me that it was a terrible idea. And yet, if he'd walked back into that room right now and kissed me, I wasn't sure that I would have been able to stop him.

I sighed and went to the bathroom to shower and take off my make-up. This whole night had been for nothing. And yet, as I stripped out of my fancy clothes and pulled off my shoes, there was the tiniest flicker of excitement in my chest as I thought about Rajesh's arm around my waist.

I would have liked it elsewhere. The thought sprang into my head from nowhere, and as soon as it was there, I couldn't help but indulge it. How would his hands feel slipping lower, across my backside, sliding between my legs? My dress was cast aside now, but I imagined how it would have felt to feel his hands stripping me down, slipping over my bare belly, drawing me close to him – his nose in my hair, inhaling the scent of me, as though he couldn't get enough. I closed my eyes for a moment; the fantasy was so real that I could almost feel his fingers against my skin.

And then the shower pounced on, alerted by my proximity, and the hot water splashed down over my body and yanked me from my fantasy. My eyes flew open, and I sighed, stepping beneath the overheated water. Maybe I should have tried for a cold shower instead.

I woke early the next morning, the taste of alcohol on my breath, and the first thing I thought of as I went to brush my barren mouth was Rajesh.

He'd shared himself with me last night. Not a lot, but enough – enough that I felt like I knew him in ways that not everyone knew him. And I'd shared things about myself that I had done so well keeping quiet up until now, things I was sure I would never tell him. Yes, the alcohol had loosened my tongue a little, but there came a point where I was so hypnotized by him that I would have told him anything he wanted to hear. It was an unsettling thought. He had so much power over me – what if he decided to exploit it?

I forced those thoughts out of my head as we went about the next day of the conference. Last night hadn't delivered what we'd needed, and with Priya's threat of redundancy hanging over both of our heads, I knew that the pressure was on when it came to delivering a story that she was happy with. We met downstairs in the lobby, and my heart flipped as soon as I laid eyes on him. How could it be that this one man could send shivers down my spine with nothing more than a glance?

"Let's do this," Rajesh greeted me, and there was tightness to his brow that told me that this was going to be deadly serious. He had to be as aware of the time-crunch we were facing as I was, and he had no time to waste. I pushed all the thoughts I'd been nurturing through the night about the two of us from my head – I needed to stay focused. My career depended on it.

We headed down to the conference – it was quieter than it had been in the days before, probably because it was too early for the people who were still nursing hangovers from the night before to be awake yet. I was feeling wide-eyed and ready to go, though it was more the nervous energy that had me on my feet instead of a good night's rest.

"What do we need to do today?" I asked, turning to him as I tucked my press pass beneath my jacket so that it wouldn't stick out. He tightened his jaw.

"We need to find something that actually confirms that the two companies are talking with each other," he sighed. "They brushed us off last night so we probably shouldn't bother with the Apollo Technologies team, but the Pritath group…"

"How are we going to prove it with neither of them here?" I pointed out, sweeping my arm across the room. He narrowed his eyes, zeroing in on a booth towards the left side of the room.

"I think I have an idea," he murmured and headed in the direction of the small, nondescript-looking booth across the hall. I hurried to keep up with him.

"What are you doing?" I asked.

"I saw the Pritath heads talking to him yesterday," he explained. "I'm hoping that if he had a slightly loose tongue with us, he might have said something to this guy that we can use."

"You really think…?" I reacted.

"It's the best we've got right now," he shot back, his voice hard around the edges. I narrowed my eyes at him and he held his hands up.

"Sorry, sorry," he apologised. "I didn't mean to snap. Let's just see if there's anything here, right?"

"Right," I agreed, and just like that, we were in front of the booth. The man behind it – short, with slightly messy hair and a crumpled shirt – lifted his chin from where it had been sitting in his hand and looked up at us. His eyes brightened as soon as he saw us, and he sprang to his feet.

"I haven't seen anyone here all day," he grinned, rubbing his hands together as though to warm them up. "How are you doing?"

"We're good, thanks," Rajesh adjusted the press pass on his front, making sure that it was visible, and the man looked shocked to see it.

"Are you guys here to do a story on me?" He immediately preened, running his hand through his hair and tilting his chin up proudly. "About the deal? I didn't realize that they were already talking about it…"

"Yes, that's right," Rajesh nodded, not missing a beat as he went along with the man's story. He glanced over at me. "Do you have a Dictaphone there?"

"I do," I pulled it from my pocket and handed it to him, beaming widely at the man sitting opposite to us, delighted that we seemed to be getting somewhere. Rajesh took the Dictaphone, clicked it on, and held it out to the man.

"So, you're…?" Rajesh paused expectantly to let the man fill in the blanks, which he did at once. He was obviously giddy with excitement over whatever it was he thought we were there to talk to him about.

"I'm Naveen Chada," he leaned far too close to the Dictaphone. "And this is my business, Carpe Chada."

"And can you explain to our readers what you do?" Rajesh prompted. I had to suppress a smile. He was doing such a good job rolling with the punches here, and I was glad that I wasn't the one behind the microphone.

"I'm working on a touch-less technology for cell phones and tablets," he explained proudly. "I came up with the idea a few years ago, and I've been perfecting it ever since."

"And you said there was a deal on the table? Would you like to tell us a little more about that?" Rajesh asked him.

"I'm not sure how much I can say, but…" Naveen eyed Rajesh for a moment, and the excitement on his face was palpable and clearly overwhelming his common sense. "You're from a big publication, right? They said they had an interview set up to announce the deal."

"We certainly are," Rajesh replied smoothly. Okay, so now we were into dangerous territory. I felt like we were treading through a field of landmines, and the only way to keep them from going off was to keep my mouth firmly and utterly shut.

"Okay, well," he took a deep breath and then shook his head. "I honestly can't believe that any of this is happening. I knew I was getting somewhere when Wolfe Tech reached out to me, but then for—"

"Wolfe Tech?" Rajesh's ears practically visibly perked up. "They were in contact with you?"

"For a little while, yes," Naveen nodded. "But when Anaya came to me at the start of the conference and offered me a deal with Apollo Tech, I wasn't going to turn it down. They're the biggest name in the business, except maybe for Pritath..."

"This deals with Apollo," Rajesh asked carefully. "Was it finalised quickly?"

"Very fast, now you mention it," Naveen frowned as though the thought had only just occurred to him. "He actually came and found me on the first day to pin me down for this deal like he knew about me. But, I suppose, people must be discussing me these days!"

"I'm sure they will be," Rajesh nodded, straight-faced, and I had to suppress a grin at the double-meaning to what he'd just said.

"Do you need a quote or something?" Naveen asked, but Rajesh waved his hand.

"I think we've got everything we need for the time being," he assured him with a smile. "Thanks for your time. And congratulations on the deal."

"No problem," Naveen beamed again. "Just let me know if you need anything else, right?"

"We certainly will," Rajesh nodded, and we backed away. As soon as we were out of earshot, I lowered my voice and spoke, "So, what does that give us?"

"A confirmation that Apollo has been trying to undermine Wolfe in more ways than one," he replied, a grin creeping up his face. "So now we just have to find a way to link this new technology with Pritath, and we've got a stone-cold connection between them."

"And how do you intend to do that?" I cocked my head at him expectantly.

"I'm going to take advantage of Gaurav's ego," he replied, and nodded in the direction of Gaurav, who was just entering the conference, looking a little worse for wear. Rajesh and I exchanged a look, and he clicked the Dictaphone on in his hand once more, but this time tucked it into his pocket.

"Are you allowed to do that?" I asked quietly, feeling like I was part of some cheesy spy movie. Maybe I should have checked to see if the hairclip I'd slid in that morning was actually a poison dart in disguise.

"Nope," he shrugged. "But we don't have to use quotes directly. I just need the gist."

Suddenly, we had caught up to Gaurav, who was alone that morning. His entourage was probably still up in bed, and what exactly he was doing there instead of sitting tucked up under the covers ordering greasy room service all day remained to be seen. He looked up at us with something close to exhaustion in his eyes, and Rajesh plastered an enormous smile as we got closer.

"Good morning," he greeted him, tucking his press pass back inside his jacket discreetly. "Good night last night?"

"I suppose you could call it that," Gaurav pinched his nose between his thumb and index finger. "I lost my wallet. I went to the desk and they said they'd look for it, but until then I'm stuck waiting around here."

"Well, it's good to run into you again," Rajesh remarked.

"You too," Gaurav agreed, and his eyes slid over to me. He looked me up and down, any apparent restraint he might have had in front of his female companion lost now that she was elsewhere. I decided to take the opportunity – maybe he'd respond better to me than to Rajesh.

"I heard last night," I lied quickly, "That there are going to be touch-less phones introduced soon."

Gaurav glanced up at me in surprise, and then raised his eyebrows.

"Well, I wouldn't know anything-"

"I heard that Wolfe Industries – have you heard of them? – I heard that they're partnering with some new company to bring them to the market," I cocked my head at him, playing as dumb as I could. It didn't come easy. "And I was just wondering, someone like you, with your kind of power, you must know something about that, right?"

"Wolfe Industries?" he bristled in distaste and maybe some combination of my flirting, his hangover, and his overinflated ego finally drew something out of him. "That's bullshit. Touch-less phones will be ours first, we just signed a—"

He cut himself off before he could go any further, rolled his shoulders back, and returned his expression to impassive.

"Trust me when I say that I know that Wolfe Industries won't be bringing out touch-less phones anytime soon," he replied, the hint of a sneer in his voice as though the very thought of it was enough to make him laugh. "But you'll see them soon enough."

"Oh, I can't wait," I nodded excitedly. "You'll have to let me know when they come out. I'm so excited."

"For you, I'd get a prototype," his eyes slid up and down my body again, and I fought the urge to shudder. There was something about being under his greasy gaze that made me want to raid the hotel supplies for soap, climb into a hot shower, and scrub until I got the feel of his eyes off me.

"Maybe we should get going," Rajesh nudged me. "We have that...?"

"Of course, yes, we have to go," I fluttered my eyelashes at Gaurav, hoping he brought the act. "But I'll see you later?"

"Just give me a call," he replied, pulling a card from his pocket and handing it to me. I took it from him and tucked it into my pocket carefully, even though I knew it was going to end up in the trash as soon as he turned his back. I wished I could stuff him and his creepy glances in there too. He turned away, and Rajesh and I exchanged a triumphant look. He grabbed me by the waist, leaned in, and murmured in my ear so Gaurav couldn't hear us.

"Back up to the hotel room," he ordered. "Now."

His mouth was so close to mine that I could have just turned my head and kissed him right then and there. For a moment, all common sense took a running jump out the window and I almost did it. I wanted nothing more than to feel his mouth on me again. If we were in a cheesy spy movie, this was the moment where he swept me up in his arms and carried me to the bedroom, and the camera would fade to black and give us our privacy. Except that I didn't want to miss a single moment of what he was going to do to me.

He pulled back, and I remembered where we were – no spy movie with a dramatic, romantic twist, but a dull conference room hall that was more suited to grey-suited tech conferences than pulse-racing romance.

We headed for the lift and he held the door for me, stepping aside so I could get in first like the true gentleman he was. I glanced over my shoulder, with something my mother might have described as a "come-hither" look, and our gazes met once more. Excitement was pulsing through my veins – both at the information we'd just uncovered and the look on Rajesh's face as the doors slid shut behind us. He paused in front of me, staring down at me, and I saw my own emotions reflected in him. I had to tear my eyes from his not to just give in and fall into his arms right there and then.

Once we were back at the room, Rajesh was all business. The moment we'd shared before vanishing just like that as he pulled out the Dictaphone and dumped it on the bed, picking up his laptop.

"What now?" I asked.

"We need to transcribe this recording," he explained, pulling up a blank document and poising his fingers over the keys, but then he glanced over to the two glasses and the bottle of champagne left forgotten after he'd left the night before. A smile curled up on his lips.

"Or," he suggested, closing the laptop and returning his attention to me. "We could… celebrate?"

"What do you mean?" I found myself asking, even though what I really should have been doing was shutting him down and reminding him how much was riding on us getting this story once and for all.

"Champagne," he replied firmly.

"You're talking like I don't have a choice," I remarked playfully, and he raised his eyebrows.

"Who says you do?" He shot back, and grabbed the phone. "Come on, I want to make the most of being here."

"And that means all room service all the time?" I said.

"Of course," he shrugged, and within a minute he'd called up a bottle of champagne so expensive my eyes practically bugged out of my head as soon as he'd ordered it.

"Isn't that too much?" I pulled a face. "Priya's already made enough at us as it is-"

"Turns out we get a free bottle with the honeymoon suite," he grinned at me. "For the newlyweds."

"So you didn't need to steal that bottle last night?" I teased. He held his hands up.

"Hey, that's just my kleptomania, that's unrelated," he protested, and then lay back on the bed. "I can't believe we actually got that out of them today. It's everything we needed."

I perched next to him, sitting up, staring off into space as my mind continued to crunch the numbers and facts that we had in hand to figure out what we could do next.

"And what now?" I replied, glancing over my shoulder at him. I felt a jolt of recognition, my mind pulling me back to that first night that we'd spent in this bed together – when I had woken to find him wound around me, his body curled around mine, his arms strong against my waist.

"We don't need to think about that right now," he assured me, sitting up so that we were eye-to-eye once more. We were so close to each other that I could smell his aftershave, see each crumple in his shirt. I reached to fix one, not giving a thought to how my actions might read, and he caught my hand in his.

My heart stopped. My breath caught in my throat, and the air around us seemed to still into nothingness as I looked up to catch his eye. This wasn't an act – this wasn't for anyone's benefit, but ours. He wanted me to know that. His gaze slid down, to my mouth, and I found that every muscle in my body was tense as I waited for him to make the next move. I couldn't do it, but he could, and he wanted to, and all I wanted in the world at that moment was for him to lean in and cover my mouth with his, and finally, finally take me.

But before he could do anything, there was a knock at the door that pulled us both from the little fantasy we'd allowed ourselves to get lost into for a moment. He dropped my hand, my skin feeling cold against the air without his touch. I clasped my hands in my lap and looked down at them accusingly as he went to get our champagne. How could I be so stupid? How could I think for a moment that this was a good idea? The trouble we would end up in wasn't worth it. Was it?

He tipped the waiter and returned with our champagne, and as he reached for the glasses, he moved to turn on the radio as well.

"Too quiet in here," he muttered. "Need some music..."

He flicked on the radio, and music filled the room. I recognised it at once, and couldn't help but giggle and put my hand to my face when I realized what it was.

"What's wrong?" He grinned, over the sounds of the smooth jazz emanating from the speakers. "Don't you like it?"

"I used to listen to this kind of thing all the time when I was a kid," I gestured to the radio, shaking my head at myself. "It's... yeah, it's a little embarrassing."

"So you've always been a romantic, then?" He teased, handing me a glass of champagne. With the music coursing through the room, it felt as though someone was stage-directing the scene, putting everything in place to make this the most romantic moment they could possibly come up with. All we needed now was the lights to dim and him to ask me to—

"Care to dance?" He bowed comically low in front of me, and I raised my eyebrows. Okay, now this was getting a little cliché – and I hated to admit that I loved every second of it. Akshay had never romanced me, not in our entire relationship, but it seemed to come easily to Rajesh, like second nature. I took a sip of the champagne, planted the glass down on the bedside table, and slipped my hand into his. What else could I do?

He pulled me close at once, a playful smile appearing on his face, and I melted against him. He had never held me like this before, at least not while he was conscious, and his body felt so natural next to mine. His gaze softened and his other hand slid around my waist, drawing me in further, until there was barely an inch between our faces. He looked even better close up, the smallest imperfections – the stubble on his jaw, the slight crookedness of his nose – only serving to make him more handsome. They were the only things that were reminding me that he was, in fact, a part of the same world as me.

He began to sway, stepping back and forth in time to the music and I did my best to keep up. I had never been much of a dancer, and I found myself tripping over my feet. He laughed good-naturedly.

"I wish I could blame it on the champagne," I glanced up at him apologetically, and his feet came to a halt so he could pull me upright once more.

"We don't have to move," he murmured, and I found my face pressed against his shoulder. He was so strong, even beneath his shirt, and something crackled to life deep inside me, something that I wasn't sure had ever been truly awake before this moment. I closed my eyes, and felt myself weaken. I was glad he was there to hold me up, because if he hadn't had his hand around my waist, I wasn't sure I could have kept myself upright.

The music filled the air around us, hiding us from the world, and for a moment, I could convince myself that all the worries and troubles that had been cluttering up my head were far away, so far away from this man in this room that they didn't matter any longer. For just one moment. But then, one moment was all it took.

Rajesh paused for a moment, and I lifted my head from his shoulder. We were staring directly at each other, and for once, he was silent. Because there was nothing else left to say.

Placing a finger on my chin to tilt my face up towards his, Rajesh leaned in slowly and planted his lips against mine. As soon as our mouths touched, the fire that had begun smouldering within me reared up, flashing behind my eyes, desire lingering across every nerve-ending on my body. This was different than the kiss back in the restaurant, which had been half for the benefit of the people around us; this was just for us, only for us, the sweetness of his mouth as he parted my lips with his tongue sending explosive shivers down my spine. The kiss deepened, the intent clear, and I arched my back to press my body against his. I just wanted to feel him against me, to feel his strength and his softness, to focus on the contradiction of those two sides of him that seemed like it would never fail to fascinate me.

I wasn't sure how long we stood in the middle of that room, holding each other, the music curling around us like smoke around our fire. It was strange, the mix of feelings within me. I didn't want this moment to end, but at the same time, I wanted more, more than I'd ever wanted from anyone before. He seemed to sense that.

Finally, he pulled back, brushing a strand of hair back from my face and smiling at me softly.

"Come with me," he murmured, and he took my hand and led me over to the bathroom. Stepping inside, he turned on the taps for the enormous bathtub that I had been avoiding up until now, and then turned his attention back to me as the steam began to fill the room.

Moving towards me, he tucked his hands beneath my hair and pulled it back, letting it flow down my back, and slid his fingers down my arms. I couldn't take my eyes off him, my body so highly sensitized to his touch that every movement felt explosive. He reached around to my front, and slowly began to unbutton my jacket, then my shirt, pulling them apart one at a time. His eyes slid down my body, and I found my breath catching in my throat. I wanted this. I wanted him to lay his eyes on me like this. I couldn't get enough.

I reached out towards him and realized that my fingers were trembling. He grinned at me, caught my hand, and brought it to his chest, where I began to slowly undo his buttons. His skin was warm beneath the fabric and he closed his eyes as though to savour the feeling of my touch so close to him. I could feel his heartbeat beginning to pick up under my fingertips, and I couldn't help but smile knowing that I was having the same effect on him that he had on me.

I pulled open his shirt, and ran my hand down his bare chest boldly. He closed his eyes, letting out a small moan, and my heartbeat picked up to match his. He let his shirt fall off his arms to the floor, and then reached over to pull off my shirt and my jacket, letting them pool at my feet. Stepping forward, he slid his arms around me again, and feeling our flesh against each other was intoxicating, more so than the champagne could ever hope to be. He quickly undid my bra and traced the straps down and off my shoulders, letting it drop to the floor, and I realized that right then and there I was more naked in front of him than I had been in front of anyone in my entire life. I wasn't scared or nervous or unsettled. It felt natural. Good. Perfect.

The steam from the bath continued to fill the room as he carried on undressing me, kneeling at my feet to undo the zip on my skirt and slowly rolling it down my legs till I was standing before him in nothing but white cotton underwear. He looked up at me, his eyes aching with desire, and I looked back down at him – and, in one swift motion, he leaned forward to plant a kiss on me through my underwear. I gasped at the sudden heat of his mouth through the fabric, but he was back on his feet before I could say anything else. The sensation of his kiss pulsed through my body, a warmth spreading out to encompass every inch of skin, and I was already desperate for more.

"The bath's run," he remarked softly, placing a hand on the small of my back and guiding me towards the enormous tub. With a deep breath, and thankful for the steam to cover my nakedness, I slipped out of my panties and slid beneath the water.

It was warm and lapped up around the tops of my arms. I closed my eyes and enjoyed the way it felt, taking deep breaths to steady myself. A strange feeling, somewhere between excitement and nervousness, swirled in my stomach, and I did my best to pay no attention to it.

With a soft splash, a fully-undressed Rajesh entered the water next to me, and I opened my eyes once more. He smiled at me and I slid towards him, moving through the water, as he reached for me and drew me onto his lap. Beneath the softly lapping waves around us, none of this felt truly real, like it had been plucked straight from a dream and dropped into my world at random.

Rajesh leaned down to kiss my neck, brushing his mouth along the sensitive spot where my ear met my throat, and I squirmed in his lap as his hands drifted up my back to cradle me softly. I moved so that our lips met once more, and again lost myself to his touch, to the feel of his body next to mine.

I wasn't sure how long we were in that bath together, but by the time he stood up and scooped me into his arms and carried me towards the bed, my entire body was gently warmed through and my skin was damp and more accustomed to his touch. The heat that had sparked to life deep inside me had grown to a flickering flame, fuelled by his touch, and by the time he laid me down on the bed, any sense of nervousness or fear I had at the thought of my first time had vanished completely. He climbed astride me, reaching up to brush a strand of damp hair from my face, and I reached up to pull him down towards me. He looked so good like this, staring down at me as though I was the only thing in the whole world he wanted, and I couldn't get enough of him. I felt as though I was addicted, wild with desire, wild with need.

"I've wanted you from the first moment I laid eyes on you," Rajesh breathed in my ear, as his hand travelled down between my legs. His deft fingers found that most sensitive part of me and I gasped, eyes flying open as he began to work his magic. My mouth opened and closed as though I was trying to find a way to put into words something that I could never have found the verbiage tc express.

He moved down, kissing across my neck and my breasts; his tongue found my nipples and he teased them both one at a time until I was squirming with need below him. He travelled further, his mouth brushing across my sensitive lower belly as he parted my thighs, and then, all at once…

"Ah!" I arched my back off the bed, eyes flying open as the shock of pleasure passed through me. His mouth was on me, in ways that I had only ever dreamed about in my deepest fantasies before this moment. The music was still playing, but I was barely aware of it, only able to pay attention to the sensations his talented tongue was sending all across my body. I squirmed beneath him, almost over-sensitized, but he slid his hands beneath my backside and drew me on to him, his mouth enveloping my wetness, and all I could do was give myself over to the delicious feelings coursing through my skin. I looked down at him and found that he was peering up at me, watching my every reaction, and the sight of his overheated eyes on me was almost enough to push me over the edge right there and then. But all at once, he eased up, softening his tongue and brushing it lightly against me, his hands moving up to caress my belly and my breasts once more. My entire body ached with need, with want, and I knew that his tongue wasn't enough to satisfy me. I needed more than this.

I reached down to pull him up on top of me once more and he kissed me again, and I could taste myself on his lips. The mixture of us in his kiss was curious and intoxicating, at once familiar and brand new. I tentatively reached down, between his legs, and wrapped my fingers around his hardness. I took a sharp breath in when I felt him, throbbing beneath my fingers. I felt an urgent need within me, something I had never felt before, but something that I recognised at once.

"I need you," I murmured into his ear as he kissed my neck once more, and he nodded, understanding at once. Slipping his hand into the drawer next to the bed, he pulled out a condom – I smiled nervously at him, glad that he had thought to cover contraception. He quickly unwrapped the condom and sheathed himself. As I looked down to watch his busy hands around his hardness, a jolt of excitement coursed through my veins. This was more than anything I'd ever felt before, way more, and with every touch it felt as though I grew more heated. The fire deep within me had blazed up to an inferno as he positioned himself over me, running his hand up my leg and gently pushing it back so he could access me. I felt him nudge up against my entrance and then, in one smooth motion, he pushed inside of me.

I gasped, and he kissed me deeply, winding his fingers through mine and pressing my hands back against the bed as he moved within me. It was an odd sensation at first, one of a kind of fullness I had never felt before, a slight pinching deep inside me as my usual two fingers weren't a match for his size. But it soon gave way to pleasure, pleasure the likes of which I had never felt before. The pleasure that was deep and profound and seemed to echo through me, dousing the fire in my belly as I finally found the relief that I had been looking for all this time. I lifted my hips up and allowed him to push deeper inside me, enjoying the way he felt, savouring it. He finally broke our kiss, our fingers still interlaced, and I took in every contour of his face as it contorted with pleasure and desire. I leaned up to brush my lips ever-so-gently against his as we made love and a smile spread out across his face at my touch. Letting go of my hands, he slipped his arms around my torso and pulled me up so that I was sitting astride him; we moved together, as though on instinct. His motions were slow and deep as we rocked back and forth together, his hands travelling over my body as though he was committing every inch of me to memory. I knew how he felt. It was as though I couldn't get close enough to him.

Slowly, something began to build in me again, with every rock of my hips. Heat radiated out from between my legs, my skin prickling and my muscles tensing as I drew closer to the edge. I pressed my face against his shoulder, inhaling the scent of him, surrounding myself with it, losing myself to it – after all this time, after all this holding back, we had finally found our release within each other and it was more than I ever could have dreamed of. He was more than I could have dreamed of. And, just like that, the feeling overwhelmed me, taking me over, like someone had struck a match deep inside me and now the flames were fluttering over my skin. I let out a cry of pleasure, tilting my head back, and Rajesh slid his hand up to cup my head and pressed his lips to my throat, his breath warm in the coolness of the room. For a moment, my head spun, and I felt as though I had been launched upward and out of the hotel room, out of the country, out of this world, as I pulsed around him. And then, I came drifting back down, my body crumpling against his as he continued to move inside me.

Moments later, through gritted teeth, Rajesh let out a growl of pleasure and found his own release inside of me. I held him close, my breath still coming fast and my heart still racing. He wrapped his arms tight around me and pulled me against him.

I could feel his breathing against my ear, feel his heartbeat as it returned to normal. It felt like we were falling back down into reality together, clutching each other as though our lives depended on it. Slowly, he pulled back and kissed once more – a soft, chaste kiss that felt oxymoronic to what we'd just done together. He lifted me off of him gently and pulled out of me, swiftly disposing of the condom, and then lay down next to me in bed. I went to pull the covers up and over my naked body, but he brushed my hands away.

"Please, just for a little longer," he murmured against my neck as he nuzzled against me. "I love seeing you like this. It's so… intimate."

I let out a long breath I didn't know I'd been holding. I supposed some part of me had been worried that after this was done, he would lose interest in me. But here he was, lying next to me and touching me and holding me and letting me know that this was far from over yet. He lay next to me, and I tentatively rested my head on his shoulder. The music was still playing, the champagne glasses forgotten. I briefly wondered what time it was, but realized that I didn't care. Nothing mattered in that moment but the sound of his steady heartbeat against my cheek, and the feel of his chest rising and falling against me. I had just shared something with this man, something I didn't know I'd ever share with anyone, but somehow it didn't feel like I'd lost anything. No, I felt like I'd gained something, my body feeling different curled around his. I felt my eyes drifting shut as the mixture of emotions crept up on me, and before I knew it, I had fallen asleep in his arms.

When I woke, my eyes drifted open slowly, and took a moment to focus on Rajesh. He was lying opposite me, his gaze soft and half-asleep, and a smile curled up on to his mouth when he saw that I was awake. He reached over to brush a strand of hair from my face and leaned across to plant a soft kiss on my forehead.

"I always wondered what it would be like waking up next to you," he murmured, running a hand down my bare arm. At some point, he must have pulled the covers up and over me, because they were covering me where they hadn't been before.

"Does it live up to the expectations?" I asked, and he grinned.

"Better than I ever could have hoped," he replied, and my heart flipped in my chest. His hand was warm on my skin, and a part of me wanted to slide across the bed towards him and go for another round of lovemaking – but I knew that no matter how much I wanted to stay hidden away in this little romantic cocoon that we'd made for ourselves, the real world wouldn't take long to come crashing in, and we still had a story to write.

I sat up and he followed suit, sliding an arm around my shoulders and pulling me against him. He pressed his nose into my hair and inhaled deeply, as though he wasn't ready to do what he knew we had to quite yet.

"We have to work," I reminded him gently, but I didn't want to break away from his embrace. He let out a small groan of dissatisfaction.

"I know we do," he grumbled playfully. "But can't we put it off for a little while longer yet?"

"And here I was thinking you were a dedicated journalist," I shot back in a faux-scolding tone.

"I am, most of the time," he protested. "Just not when there's a beautiful girl in my bed next to me."

"And if I get out of bed?" I asked mischievously.

"Then you'll be even more distracting," he ran a hand down my bare thigh suggestively.

"We really should get to work," I replied, a little disappointed that we couldn't just spend the rest of the day in bed together, doing nothing but touching and caressing and learning each other's bodies off by heart. But if we didn't get this story together, then we would have all too much time to laze around doing nothing, because we'd be out of our jobs.

"Well, if we have to work, there's no one I'd rather be working with than you," he grinned, heading back through to the bathroom to grab his clothes and quickly throwing on his underwear and trousers. I went to do the same, pulling on my underwear and bra, and turned to find him watching me from across the room.

"What are you looking at?" I flushed, very aware of how naked I was, but he stepped towards me and wound his arms around me.

"Just a woman I never thought I'd get to see like this," he murmured against my shoulder, kissing my collarbone briefly and sending a shiver down my spine. "I've never..."

He trailed off, as though not sure he should say what was on his mind. But I had to hear it.

"You never...?"

"I've never felt this way about someone before, Prisha," he finished up, our eyes meeting in the bathroom mirror opposite us. His gaze was burning with sincerity, and for a moment, it felt as though my heart had stopped beating in my chest. He meant what he was saying.

"Everything is different when you're around," he went on, as though a dam had burst and he could finally share everything that he had been bottling up all this time. "You're...it felt like something clicked into place when we met, but I didn't realize what it was back then. But now..."

"You do?" I breathed. I knew how he felt. Our bodies wrapped around each other's like this, it felt as though we made up two halves of the same whole, as though my life before him had been leading to this moment as though this was inevitable. The two of us had been barrelling towards this moment all along, even if we hadn't known it, our entire lives headed to crash straight into each other. And now that we were here, the thought of what came next was equal parts thrilling and terrifying. Because I had never felt this deeply for someone before, this cavernous feeling that seemed to ache inside me, a love for him so fierce it was as though my entire body was bursting with it. All I could do was turn to plant my lips against his – for once. I couldn't find the words to say what I knew I needed to. But I would. I would spend my life searching for them if I had to, but I would.

He unfurled himself from around me and drew himself back up, taking a deep breath as though cleansing himself.

"Okay, we need to get that work done," he grinned at me, but with his touch all thoughts of work had vanished from my head. I had to blink twice to remind myself where I was and what I was doing here, and then reached for my Dictaphone.

We spent the rest of the afternoon transcribing what we had and arranging it as part of the evidence we had already gathered over the course of the last few weeks. We actually had a story now – something solid, something concrete, and something that might keep Priya from firing us as soon as we got back to the office. But we were still missing an important hook, that exclusive angle that would pull people into the story. Rajesh paced back and forth as I read out to him what we had once more, and shook his head.

"We're not quite there yet," he grimaced.

"But what else do we need?" I pointed out. "Unless we can get one of them to confess to what they're doing straight up, I don't know what we can do."

"Any thoughts on how to get someone to admit to their wrongdoing while we record it?" He grinned at me wryly, raising his eyebrows expectantly. I sank back into the bed, letting out a long sigh.

"I have no idea," I admitted. "So what do we do now?"

"We go back down to the conference tomorrow and see what we can find out," he replied firmly. "I know we can find what we need."

"I'm glad someone does," I muttered because there was something else playing at the back of my mind too, now that we'd finally given in to our feelings for each other. Now we had to convince Priya that we had not only gone off and used her resources to cover a story that she had never approved, but that we were involved with each other. Rajesh seemed to figure out what was bothering me at once, and he sat next to me on the bed and caught my chin in his hand.

"Hey," he said softly, and I tilted my eyes up to meet his tiredly.

"I know it's going to be rough when we get back," he admitted. "Really rough. And I know that Priya isn't going to be happy about this-"

"She could fire us," I pointed out bluntly.

"I don't care if she does," he replied and now it was my turn to raise my eyebrows at him.

"I'm sorry, I'm sorry," he squeezed my hand. "I know you actually want to keep this job."

"Yeah, I do," I nodded. "So what are we going to do about… us?"

"Uh, claim this was all research for the story?" He suggested jokingly, but I couldn't find it in me to offer much more than a chuckle. He swept a strand of hair back from my face; it was as though he couldn't get enough of touching me, determined to commit every inch of me to memory. As though that's all he might have to rely on in the near future.

"We can worry about that once we've got the story," he replied firmly. "And if it comes to it, I'll quit."

"You'll quit?" My mouth hung open in shock.

"I'll quit," he nodded. "There are other jobs going for me out there and I..."

He looked deep into my eyes, and for a moment the world swam wildly around me as everything focused in on the look he was giving me.

"I don't want to give this up," he murmured, brushing his thumb lightly over my lips. "Everything's better when you're around, Prisha. I'm not walking away from that."

"Hopefully it won't come to that," I protested weakly, but my heart was leaping up and down in my chest at the knowledge that he would go that far for me.

"Hopefully," he agreed, a grin on his face. "Come on, let's get a plan in place. We can't worry about getting back to the office when we've still got a story to find here."

Okay. I could do this.

I took a deep breath and my shoulders sank once more. I couldn't do this.

"It's going to be alright," Rajesh nudged me. "Really, I believe in you."

"That's nice, but I don't believe in me," I groaned. "Are you sure you can be there for it? It would probably be better if—"

"Trust me, you need to do this yourself," Rajesh assured me. "It's the only way you can be sure."

I pressed my lips together and furrowed my brow. This was a last-ditch attempt, the only thing we'd been able to come up with to address the void that was still left in our story after we got the scoop from the vendor. With time running out at the conference, we knew we had to do big or go home – and man, were we going huge.

"You ready?" He raised his eyebrows at me, pressing the Dictaphone into my hand. I nodded.

"As I'll ever be," I muttered, and he went for the door.

"You can do this," he assured me. And I knew what he meant was – you have to do this. Because this was the only thing we'd been able to come up with to make our story stick, and even this felt like the longest shot.

Rajesh ducked out and left me in the room by myself, and I sat on the bed and crossed and uncrossed my legs uncomfortably. This was like hell. There was no other way to put it. Sitting in this room, waiting for the one man I'd hoped I would never have to see again.

There was a knock at the door, and my head snapped up. Please let that be Rajesh because he'd forgotten something. I got shakily to my feet, pulled the door open, and found myself faced with Akshay. His eyes widened as his gaze fell on me and I attempted to look as pulled-together and normal as possible.

"Hey," I greeted him, even though it felt as though someone was churning butter in my insides. Why had I agreed to this again?

Well, because Akshay was working with Pritath Industries, and he was the only direct connection we had to the business. And when I had let slip to Rajesh that Akshay, who he'd spotted out and about with Gaurav a couple of times, was an old acquaintance of mine, he insisted on setting up this interview.

"Are you kidding me?" My eyes practically bugged out of my head and Rajesh nodded.

"If you actually know him, maybe he'll tell you something that he wouldn't share with someone else," he pointed out. I hadn't even known what he was here for before that moment, but Rajesh had asked around and managed to pull some new employment files from a few of the people he knew in the industry and could confirm that yes, it was Akshay and yes, he was working with one of the businesses we needed an inside track on.

"I really don't think he wants to see me."

"We won't tell him who's interviewing him," Rajesh went on excitedly. "We'll just drop the name of The Chronicle and he'll come running. They always do when you dangle a little publicity in their faces."

I thought back to the book that Akshay had kept of all the newspaper clippings and stories that featured either him or the companies he'd worked for in them and felt something sag inside me. Because I knew Rajesh was right. He would come running.

We'd set up the meeting, making sure that Akshay had no idea who was interviewing him, and invited him up to the hotel room to get him away from the rest of the group he was with. We needed him separated from the pack, more likely to drop some information that the people around him would probably do their best to talk over or contradict so we didn't find anything out. Akshay was arrogant as hell, and I knew if I could just appeal to those sensibilities within him, then I could get what we needed.

And now, I found myself standing in front of him, looking up at him, the familiar contours of his face and smell of his thick, overly heavy aftershave hanging in the air between us. I fought the urge to grimace; it was just a natural reaction to being around someone as slimy as him.

He looked down at me for a moment, and a furrow appeared in his brow.

"What the hell are you doing here?" He demanded, peering into the room as though he expected someone to spring out at any moment. "I thought I had a meeting with a reporter in here."

"I'm—" I was about to proudly announce to him that actually I was that reporter that he was meeting with, but I realized all at once that I would be better off letting him believe I was nothing more than his annoying ex turned up out of the blue again. I took a deep breath, flicked the Dictaphone on in my hand, and tucked it into my pocket.

"Is that Rajesh you're talking about?" I cocked my head at him, playing dumb. "Oh, he's my boyfriend. He just stepped out. He'll be back any minute."

"He stepped out?" Akshay seemed pissed at the thought that someone might not value his time as much as he clearly did. And then, as though reversing back over the sentence, his brow furrowed. "Your boyfriend?"

"Yes, that's right." I shrugged, blinking up at him and playing as dumb as I knew he'd always hoped I'd be. "He should be back any minute. Do you want to…?"

I let my eyes play on his lips for a moment, even though looking at them made me feel a little sick.

"…come in?"

His eyes lit up and I knew at once what was going through his brain. The fact we had never had sex was a big deal to him, and he had often pushed me to do more than I was comfortable with. I had usually been good at shutting him down, but it still annoyed me no end. And something about me flirting with him while I was dating another man (or at least, as far as he knew) would appeal to the childish competitive side of him. He stepped over the threshold.

"So, how long have you been at the conference?" I asked, twirling a strand of hair around my finger. He shrugged.

"Oh, not long," he puffed his chest out. "I'm just here with my new employers. They're pretty amazing. Maybe you'd heard of them? Pritath Industries?"

"I think that rings a bell," I wrinkled my nose up, playing dumb. "You work for them? What do you do?"

"I'm helping manage a new deal they're striking with a company," he boasted, tilting his chin up as though I was blessed to just be in conversation with him at that moment.

"What company?" My instincts kicked in and I could hear Rajesh pressing me to get more out of him. The soles of my feet prickled with excitement. I could do this. And I could see why Rajesh always seemed to find it so thrilling.

"Oh, I don't know if I can say," he shook his head, and he took a step towards me, looking down at me with a familiar glint in his eye. "How long did you say your… uh, boyfriend was going to be away for?"

"I don't know," I breathed, hoping that he would take the drop in my voice for desire and not for the disgust that it was actually concealing. "Why?"

"You've just…" He shook his head, looking me up and down. "There's something different about you. I can't put my finger on it."

"You too," I remarked, even though there was nothing different about him; he was just as arrogant and difficult as he'd ever been, and I could feel it coming off of him in waves. The way he was looking at me, his eyes roaming across my body as though he believed he already had rights to it, made me want to jerk away from him in disgust.

"I saw you around a couple of times," I confessed, deciding I could spin my story into something a little more appealing to his ego. "And I was thinking about you…"

"If I'd seen you like this, I'd have been thinking about you too," he murmured, not taking his eyes off my chest. I fought the urge to shudder, and continued speaking.

"I like my boyfriend a lot," I sighed as his hand twitched up like he wanted to lay it on me. "He's so successful. I like the kind of lifestyle he can offer me..."

"I'm a success too, you know," he replied, irritated. His jaw tightened. "With this new job..."

"Pritath Industries are one thing," I shrugged. "But there are other big companies too. It's not like you work for any of them—"

"Apollo Tech!" Akshay spread his hands out wide. "How do you like them?"

"What about them?" I pressed, forcing myself to keep focused on the task at hand, because there was so much at stake right then.

"We're making a deal with them," he boasted, his voice getting louder as though he wanted everyone to hear. "You know who they are, right? Well, I've been a major driving force behind getting us in with them, and we're going to be working with them soon, and it's going to be huge."

"Oh my god," I gasped. "That's amazing. You're so..."

I trailed off, partly because I wanted him to keep talking and partly because I didn't trust myself not to fill out the end of that sentence with a series of insults. He took a step towards me, his smile widening, and I fought the urge to duck away from him in distaste, but stood my ground. I had what I needed – but I knew that I could draw more out of him. He put his hand on my waist, mistaking my silence for some kind of acquiescence to what he so clearly wanted.

"Are you here with someone else?" I pressed, suddenly remembering the woman's bag that had been sitting out when I spotted him at dinner on the first night. He shook his head.

"No one like you," he murmured, his voice comically low, as though he'd seen someone doing it to act sexy in a film one time and had decided that was the be-all and end-all in seduction. I fought the urge to flinch. He stroked his finger across my waist. My immediate reaction was to shove him off, but I took a deep breath to steady myself, which he seemed to take as a sign of my overwhelming desire for him. How far could I push this? Because I felt as though I was going to throw up as it was. I wanted Rajesh, and only Rajesh, and with every touch Akshay was landing on me was underlining that for me.

"Someone who's a part of the business?" I pressed, sliding away from him. "You know I can't ask you to betray them like that…"

"No one who's part of business," he shook his head. "Come on, it's not betrayal; it's just putting unfinished business to bed…"

"Why are you doing the deal?" I asked, avoiding his gaze for a little longer. "I thought they were meant to hate each other, those two businesses. It doesn't make sense…"

"It was my idea," he boasted, and even though I knew he was lying, I managed to keep my face straight and my eyes wide as though what he was telling me was blowing my mind. "There's a new business come up, Wolfe Industries. And we're going to put them out of business with the new deal we're making. That's why it's so quiet, for now."

"But you know you can trust me," I replied, looking into his eyes and hoping my words were reading as sincere. He nodded, gaze softening, and I managed to offer him a smile.

He leaned down to kiss me, trying to pull me close against him, and I ducked my head out of the way on instinct. I couldn't keep the wrinkle of distaste from my nose and he finally seemed to notice that, for some reason impossible to comprehend to him, I wasn't falling over myself to fall back into bed with him.

"What's wrong?" He demanded, furrowing his brow. "Don't you want this?"

I looked up at him, the man who I had been destined to marry only a few months before, the man whose abandonment of me had torn my life apart at the seams. At this man who was making it very, very clear that he wanted me, that he was willing to do pretty much anything to get me in bed once more. The man who was jealous that I was with someone new, the man who my family approved of, the man who they'd wanted me to be with, the man who, on paper, was completely perfect for me. And I realized with a start that I didn't feel anything for him.

"No, I don't," I took a step back from him. I had gotten everything I needed to get out of him and I wasn't going to entertain this nonsense any further. His face dropped, and something close to realization dawned across his face. I reached into my pocket and pulled out my Dictaphone, waving it triumphantly in front of his face.

"I'm the reporter you were meeting," I shot in his direction, taking pleasure in proving him so utterly and completely wrong about me. "That was me. And you just told me everything that we need to know to get this story."

"What story?" His face drained of colour, the confidence leaking out of him like a pricked balloon.

"The story about this deal that you're making," I threw back. "You really think your bosses are going to be happy with this… with you telling me?"

Akshay reached towards me and tried to snatch the Dictaphone out of my hand, but I stepped back.

"You always underestimated me," I snapped, tightening my grip around the Dictaphone. "You always thought I would drop everything to come running to you, and look where that got you."

"You're a bitch," he spat in my direction, and the fury in his voice took me aback, but I stood my ground. "You're going to ruin me."

"I guess you should have thought of that before you let that thing between your legs make your decisions for you," I tightened my jaw and stood tall. "Now get the hell out before I call security."

I didn't really have any security to call, but it was enough to get him glancing around nervously as though my goons were about to jump out from behind a door and drag him away. He had always been a physical coward, and I could practically see the sweat of panic appearing on his brow. He backed to the door.

"You won't get away with this." He warned me in a last-ditch attempt to get me to give in. I shrugged.

"Neither will you," I waved the Dictaphone at him once more, reminding him what he'd confessed to me only moments before, and he went for the door and hurried out down the corridor. My heart was pounding in my chest and my stomach was churning, but it was done. We had what we needed to make the story stick. That was all that mattered. And I'd stuck it to Akshay once and for all. I slumped back against the bathroom door, feeling as though my legs were about to drop out from underneath me.

The door opened, and Rajesh burst in. He wrapped his arms around me and pulled me close, holding me up, and making sure I didn't drop to my knees right there and then.

"Are you okay?" He demanded, leaning in and peering at me intently. "I just saw Akshay running out of here."

"We got what we needed," I assured him, a smile finally breaking out across my face.

"Does he know?" Rajesh glanced over his shoulder, and I nodded, only just realizing that I perhaps shouldn't have told him what I was going to do with the newfound information. But sticking it to him like that had been so viscerally satisfying, I wasn't sure if I would have changed anything about how I acted.

"Shit," Rajesh muttered, the first time I'd really heard him curse. "Okay, that means we need to get the story in fast. How quickly can you transcribe what you got?"

"Give me half an hour," I replied, and grabbed for my computer. Blood was pulsing through my head, so loud I could almost hear it, and I grinned to myself as I booted up the computer. I had done it. We had done it. And even though I was freaking out at the thought of what came next, I would take that victory for now.

"That's it, sent," Rajesh hit the button that would deliver the article we'd just finished to Priya once and for all. He flopped back on the bed and stared up at the ceiling, before letting his eyes drift shut and releasing a breath that it sounded like he had been holding all day.

"Thank god for that," I replied, stretching and getting to my feet to stretch my legs. "That was a nightmare."

"It's not the last time you'll have to stay up all night to get a story in on time," Rajesh remarked, the flicker of a smile appearing on his face.

"Sure, but it won't be because I was stupid enough to reveal to a source that we're not exactly producing favourable coverage on him," I pointed out. I was right to feel iffy about having told Akshay what was going on, no matter how deeply satisfying it had seemed at the time. He had run back to Gaurav and apparently told him what we were planning, because he contacted Priya to threaten her about the story. Akshay had revealed the information to us without too much prompting, there wasn't a lot he could do but try and get the story to the press before we did, but that involved a careful reveal strategy that would take at least a day to put together. So we had to stay up all night long to get the story to Priya before the morning and make sure she could fit it into the morning issue of The Chronicle. We had proofread, reworked, and edited the story all night long, and now we were finally, finally finished.

I felt oddly light and free with the story finally out of our hands, even though I knew I should have been worrying about what Priya would think of it. After all, if it wasn't up to her standards, then she might still get rid of us for everything we'd tried to pull over the last few weeks. Maybe it was the sleep deprivation, but I was confident that our story would stick. I was proud of what we'd produced. Hell, I wouldn't have let Rajesh send it unless I was totally sure that it was the best thing we could have written. And I was.

I turned to him, looking at the man on the bed in front of me. We hadn't done anything physical since that day with the champagne and everything, and I was starting to wonder if he was beginning to regret it. Because he seemed to be avoiding me a little bit, drawing back – maybe it was to do with how much trouble we would have wound up in if we were found out, or maybe he was just distracted by the story, but I was starting to wonder if his feelings for me weren't as strong as I had initially thought they were.

"So, what do we do now?" I asked nervously. He lifted his head up, stretched, and yawned.

"We get some sleep," he replied firmly. "And then we get out of here before Gaurav and Apollo can send hit men after us or something.

"You really think that might happen?" My eyes widened.

"I wouldn't put it off the table," he replied gravely, and then looked up at me and laughed. "Prisha, it's okay. I'm just joking."

"Don't tease me about stuff like that!" I protested weakly, relieved to hear that I wasn't in the crosshairs of some underground contract killer as we spoke. "I haven't slept; my cognitive functions aren't working at their best."

"Let's get some rest," He suggested. "Come on."

I sat gingerly on the bed next to him and looked over at him. Inside, I was willing him to reach over and pull me close, to bury his nose in my hair and remind me just how much he wanted me all those days ago. But he didn't; he lay down and closed his eyes, and a moment later was lost to sleep once more. I did the same thing, and soon found myself drifting off next to him.

I woke up a few hours later, and found him climbing out of the shower. I smiled at him blearily, and he smiled back. I noticed his eyes travel quickly up and down my body, and felt a glimmer of excitement deep in my stomach.

"How are you?" I asked shyly, hoping that he could tell what I was asking about. He shrugged.

"Tired," he replied. "Have you heard anything from Priya yet?"

I opened up my laptop to check my email.

"No, nothing," I shook my head. "Nothing yet."

"I guess no news is good news?" He shrugged, and began towelling his hair off. He was wearing a laid back t-shirt and jeans, and somehow looked even hotter than he normally did when he was dressed up in smart slacks and a shirt. I couldn't take my eyes off him, but he seemed to be avoiding my gaze, as though facing me was something he couldn't quite bring himself to do right then.

"Is everything okay?" I asked a little disgruntled. I had shared something with him that I had never shared with anyone else, that I didn't want to share with anyone else, and now he was pulling away from me. It felt like we'd been through so much together in the preceding few weeks and now he was acting as though he barely knew me.

"What are you talking about?" He asked, challenging me to come out in the open about it. I took a deep breath. I had done well confronting the things I didn't want to in the last day, and I didn't see why this should be any different.

"You've been pulling away from me," I pointed out. "And I don't know why. After we…"

I waved my hand over the bed, still not quite able to speak the words out loud, and he nodded, understanding at once.

"After we did that, you seemed so happy to be with me," I looked at my hands, feeling a little arrogant for even saying it out loud. "And then you just…"

I let the unspoken words hang in the air between us, unsure of how to give them shape. He looked up at me, grimaced, and put his head in his hands.

"Don't you want to be with me?" I asked, trying to keep my voice light, but the weight of what was unfolding felt as though it was weighing me down, dragging me under. "I understand—"

"I want to be with you," he got to his feet suddenly, taking my hands and clasping them between his. "I do. But… I'm scared, Prisha."

"What are you scared of?" I gaped at him. How could Rajesh be scared of anything? He was the boldest, brightest, most passionate person I'd ever met, and the thought of anything even remotely unsettling him felt almost laughable in how ridiculous it seemed.

"I've been in love before," he murmured, not looking up at me as he spoke. "I've felt deeply for people, I have. But never anything close to what I feel for you."

"And that's a bad thing?" I cocked my head at him, confused.

"No, no," he shook his head. "It's a beautiful thing. This is… it's the most certain I've felt about anything in my life."

"Then what's the problem?" I breathed, not certain I wanted to hear the answer, but knowing that I had to.

"I got hurt those other times I fell for people," he explained. "One time in particular. The last woman I dated, I really dated, and it didn't end… well."

"And?" I was waiting him to finish.

"And if it was that bad ending things with her, I can't imagine how much worse it's going to be if things don't work out between us," his eyes were blazing with a range of emotions, cycling through them so fast that I couldn't put my finger on one specific feeling.

"And there's so much working against us," he continued, as if I needed reminding of the odds that were standing between us being together. "I just…"

He trailed off again. I had never heard Rajesh so short on words before. But I knew exactly how he felt; sometimes, when I was around him, it was as though something had wiped my brain off everything, but the ability to focus in on him. So, I did the only thing that I could think of – I leaned in to kiss him.

As soon as our lips touched, I swear I felt something close to relief pass across my brain. I hadn't realized just how much

I needed him until that moment. For a moment, he held back, his body stiff against mine, as though he was trying to hold back and keep himself back from me, but within a second he gave in, moaning against my lips and wrapping his arms tight around me. I loved the feeling of him next to me, his soft lips against mine, his tongue deftly parting my lips and flicking the match to light the fire between my legs once more. But I wanted to prove to him how much I wanted him – how much I was committed to making this work, to him, to the desire that pulsed in the air between us every moment we were together. I fell to my knees, between his legs, and reached up to undo his trousers.

He brushed my hands away, unzipping his trousers and stroking my hair back from my head. He didn't take his eyes off me as I slipped my hand beneath the fabric of his underwear, and found him already hard. I sucked in a sharp breath, the flames flickering deep in my belly as my desire mounted for him and grew more intense. With a deep breath, I leaned in, and took him into my mouth.

I had never done anything like that before in my life. I moved slowly, stroking my tongue back and forth and using my hands to cover the space that my mouth couldn't take. I loved the feel of his warm skin between my lips, of the sound of his soft moans and groans coming from above me. Eventually, I opened my eyes and watched him, loving the way he reacted to my every touch. For the last week-and-a-half, I'd done nothing but let him take control, let him take the lead, and followed his every move. But now, I was the one in control, and it was intoxicatingly good.

I wasn't sure how long I pleasured him with my mouth, but I knew I could have gone on all day like this. The way his jaw tightened and his eyes drifted shut to fully give himself over to the pleasure I was bringing him was one of most painfully sexy things I'd ever seen in my life. But after a while, he reached down to pull me to my feet, kissing me once more, deeper than before. I could feel the urgency in his embrace and knew that I was ready for more.

He guided me backwards towards the bed, slowly pushing my skirt back and hooking his fingers around my underwear to pull them down. The feel of his fingertips stroking down my thighs was enough to draw a heady moan from between my lips, and he reached for a condom to sheath himself swiftly. His lips met mine again and I groaned, squirming on the bed beneath him. This time, I knew exactly what I wanted from him, needing him inside me, desperate to feel the sensation of him pushing into me the way he had only a few nights before. After everything that had happened, it felt like we were teetering on the edge of a release, of finally confirming the feelings that we had worked so hard to pretend weren't there. And he didn't seem to want to wait any longer than I did, gripping my hips, pulling me roughly down the bed, and placing himself at my entrance, and then he entered me.

"Ah!" I cried out, my fingers digging into his still-clothed back. The last time this had happened, it had been romantic and slow and passionate, with both of us savouring every second of it. But this time, it was urgent and hungry and needful, both of us desperate to prove that what we felt for each other was real and undeniable.

We both moved fast, our hands and tongues and bodies moving in perfect time with one another. The bed shifted beneath us and the pleasure in my body began to circle and build, my skin prickling and my body tensing beneath his as his hands slid up my thighs to sink into my backside and pull me on to him. I hooked my ankles behind his back once again, pulling him in deep, loving the feeling of him, addicted to it. I had no idea how much I had been craving for him until that moment, until my body couldn't take any more.

"Oh..." I groaned as the orgasm swept through me, my body trembling as he covered my mouth with his once more. Our tongues met lazily, intertwining, as he pushed himself all the way into me and finished. His body relaxed against mine, his hands slipping beneath my shoulders so he could pull me in close and kiss my neck. His breath was hot and brisk, but soon slowed down, his heartbeat returning to normal as I rubbed my hand all up and down his back, loving the feel of his muscles under his shirt. I couldn't believe we'd just done that.

He pulled out of me slowly, disposing of the condom before rolling back on to the bed to draw me against his chest. But I propped myself on my elbow and looked him in the eyes.

"I need you to tell me that we can make this work," I murmured, pressing my finger to his chin so I could turn his head and get him to look into my eyes.

"What if things go wrong?" He asked, a dark cloud passing across his face. I shook my head.

"Then they go wrong," I implored him. "But put your trust in us and we'll not fail. We've already overcome so much. You really think there's anything else the world can throw at us that we can't take?"

He looked at me, and it was as though the sun was peeping through the sky after a storm. Like something was finally clearing after we had spent so long with the world trying to pull us apart, he finally believed in our ability to hold on to each other, no matter what was thrown at us.

"Prisha," he traced his thumb across my mouth, and I felt a sudden swell of emotion fill up my chest. Just the sound of my name on his lips – it was enough. Enough for what, I wasn't sure, but I felt nothing but complete and utter peace at the sound of it.

"My life wasn't right without you," he murmured. "I wasn't sure what was missing, but..."

He looked deep into my eyes and then leaned forward to plant a soft kiss on my forehead, pulling me against him and breathing in deeply, like he was committing the scent of me to memory for good.

"You were," he whispered when he was done. "You were what was missing. I see that now."

I felt my throat constrict as I feared that I might burst into tears at his words. I knew exactly what he was trying to convey. Because yes, I was scared, and yes, I had no idea what was coming next, but I knew that I wanted to share it with him, no matter how difficult it made my life. I didn't know what to say to him to convey that, but he just leaned forward and pressed his forehead against mine and I knew that he understood. There was no need for words. The only thing I needed was him.

"What are we going to tell Priya?" I fretted aloud as we packed our things and prepared to check out of the hotel for good. It was the morning after we'd put in the story, and we were leaving to head back to Delhi. I was looking forward to heading home, but I was still nervous about what would happen once we arrived back and had to deal with the fallout of our budding romance in the real world, instead of sequestered up in this hotel together where we could pretend that what happened outside these walls didn't matter.

"We'll figure it out when we get to her," Rajesh replied, wrapping his arms around my waist. We had shared a bed the night before, and he had held me tight all night long, as though he didn't want to let go of me. It seemed as though he was over his freak-out from the day before, when we had made love once more. Every time I looked at him as we were getting ready to go, I felt that uptick in my chest, the one that told me that this was the beginning of something seriously special.

"Whatever you say," I agreed, and he offered me his arm.

"Let's make the most of her not being around for the time being though, huh?" He suggested, and I cocked my head at him, not comprehending.

"What do you mean?"

"I mean, let's actually be a couple in public while we still can," he explained, that gorgeous, entrancing glint in his eye. I didn't need telling twice. I tucked my hand through his arm and he grinned at me, leaning over and planting a big, over-the-top kiss on my lips.

"Got everything?" He asked, and I nodded, hooking my bag over my shoulder.

"Ready when you are," I agreed, feeling a flutter of nervousness as we headed out the hotel room door. In theory, nothing had changed to anyone who might have been observing us all this time – we were still just some couple hanging around at this conference together. But what they didn't know is that now, we were actually together. This relationship would last after we walked out of the hotel doors, no matter how hard we had to work to keep it afloat.

We were in the lobby, waiting for the cab, when I saw her again. My stomach dropped as soon as I set eyes on her – what was it about us running into exes these last few days? Rajesh rolled his eyes as he spotted Lena, the ex we'd bumped into at the airport, striding in our direction. I squinted at her for a moment – she was carrying a bag, one that I recognised from somewhere. Maybe I had a similar one at home that I'd forgotten about?

"Don't worry, I'll handle this," he promised me, brushing his lips across my cheek as he did so, and I felt my stomach warm with confidence in him. I knew he wouldn't let anything happen to us. She arrived in front of us, far from the pulled-together, in-control woman we'd bumped into at the airport a few weeks previously.

"Morning," Rajesh nodded at her, but she ignored his greeting and looked between us.

"So, it's true, then?" She remarked, cocking an eyebrow at us both. "You're actually together?"

I glanced over at Rajesh and found that he was already looking back at me. It was clear neither of us was sure whether or not we should tell her. It was one thing for people in the hotel to know that we were together; it was a whole other beast if someone working in the same industry as us found out about us.

"Don't bother denying it," she sneered, and there was a glint of triumph in her eyes as though she was satisfied with what she'd just found out. "Glad that I know for sure one way or the other."

"How did you know?" Rajesh snapped, obviously irritated by the way she was lording it over us, and she shrugged, half-nonchalant, but unable to hide the rage that was simmering just below the surface.

"You remember Akshay, right?" She turned her attention to me, and I blinked a couple of times as his name caught me off-guard.

"Of course I do," I replied. "Why?"

"Then you know that you just ruined his entire career," she threw her hands in the air. "I hope you know that. For someone you were meant to have loved—"

"It's not our fault that he spilled the beans like that," I replied firmly. "Why does it matter to you, anyway? Surely someone ruining their career like that is a good story for someone like you—"

And suddenly, I placed where the bag had come from, where I recognised it from. The first night we were here, when I saw Akshay out at dinner, that had been the bag sitting beneath the table opposite him. The bag of the woman he was on that date with. My jaw slowly swung open as it all sank in – this was why she'd been so keen to prove us wrong. She had double the reason to hate me. Not only was I dating her ex, but she was dating mine – and she must have realized by then that I was the one who had pulled off the better deal.

"You're with him, aren't you?" I gasped, the words coming out of me slowly. Rajesh's eyes widened and he turned his gaze back to Lena for confirmation. There were tears glistening in her eyes, and she dashed them away angrily with the back of her hand.

"And you ruined him," she spat angrily in my direction. "Don't you see that? You ruined him for your stupid story."

She paused for a moment, collecting herself, and I thought we had heard the worst of her accusations. She tilted her head up, eyes still shining with tears, and forced herself to continue.

"Did you really think I was going to let you get away with that?" She murmured, and I felt a cold wash of fear pass over my body.

"What the hell are you talking about?" Rajesh demanded, his mind clearly jumping to the same place mine had. "What have you done, Lena?"

"Akshay told me that his ex was dating the guy she came here with," she remarked, a cruel smiling curling up on to her lips. "And I happen to know that The Chronicle has a rule about not allowing any inter-employee relationships."

My stomach dropped to my shoes, and clouds plagued the edge of my vision as the panic set in. She couldn't have. Could she? Would she have gone that far?

"I still have some contacts over at The Chronicle," she went on, her voice shaking but certain. "So I gave Priya a call. Turns out she was very interested to hear about your little fling."

"What the hell have you done?" Rajesh exploded, loud enough that the entire room seemed to turn around at once to see what the commotion was all about. "Lena, you could have—"

"You think I give a damn about what you think of me now?" She threw her hands in the air, cutting him off, her voice taking on a manic edge that I had never heard from her before. "You ruined the man I'm dating, Rajesh. And after everything you did to me—"

"Lena, I was wrong to treat you that way, and I know that now," Rajesh cut her off urgently. "But you can't truly believe that this is the way to fix that. You have to see that an eye for an eye is only going to end up—"

"Lena," I wasn't going to let Rajesh dig us any deeper into this hole than we already were. "Lena, I need you to listen to me for a moment."

She turned her attention to me, with complete and utter disdain on her face. I didn't blame her. In her position, I would have felt the same way.

"Akshay, yesterday…" I began, not sure how to phrase this in the way that would hurt her the least. "…he tried to seduce me. Did he tell you that?"

Her face dropped, and it was clear that my announcement was news to her. She shook her head slowly.

"No, he can't have," she protested weakly. "He would never do that to me. He—"

"He did," I went on. "I have the recordings. I can show them to you, if you like. I can show you that he tried to get me into bed."

It looked as though the last vestiges of strength had been knocked from her, like I had delivered the final blow against her. Her shoulders sagged, and for a second I was worried she was going to crumple down onto the floor in front of me. But she eventually straightened back up and looked me in the eye once more.

"Why are you telling me this?" She demanded, her voice hoarse and withered, like something in her had curled up and rotted.

"Because Akshay is not a good man," I implored her. "He's only going to use you and hurt you. He'll never accept you for who you are right now. He wants a woman who's going to stay at home and raise children and forget about her career. Trust me, he might not be showing it now, but that's what he wanted from me, and he'll expect that from you, too, at some point."

She stared at me, and I could see the flicker of comprehension in her eyes that told me that this wasn't news to her. He must have hinted at something like this before. This wasn't the first time these thoughts had crossed her mind, I was sure of it.

"I don't know you," I went on, reaching out to squeeze her arm. "But I know that you deserve better than that. I'm sure you believe that too, don't you?"

She managed to nod, and the tears began to spill down her cheeks. I removed my hand and looked over at Rajesh, who was watching me, open-mouthed.

"I think we should get out of here," I remarked, glancing over at Lena. Part of me wanted to stay and comfort her, and another part of me was all too aware that this woman who I had just shown some kindness to had very likely just ended my career with my dream employer. Rajesh nodded, and I hitched my bag up and over my shoulder and headed out to the door.

"I can't believe you just did that," Rajesh murmured as he hurried after me. I glanced around to see Lena wiping away her tears and turning to leave, hopefully to find Akshay and tell him that things were over between them. I wished I could have seen his face when she dumped him, but we had a flight to catch.

"I couldn't let him do to her what he did to me," I explained "I'm mad at her, but not nearly as mad as I am at him. She deserved to know."

"Well, you're kinder than I would have been in the circumstances," he glanced over his shoulder and then held the door for me so I could go through ahead of him. "I'm not sure I would have found the kindness in me to do that."

"It was the only constructive thing I could think of doing." I shrugged, replying honestly, and he suddenly pulled me into a tight embrace. He pressed his face against my hair and sighed deeply, and then let go. I raised my eyebrows at him.

"What was that in aid of?"

"You're just…" He looked at me for a moment. "People like you don't come around so often, Prisha. I want you to know that I realize that."

"I'll make sure to keep reminding you any chance I get," I teased, and he took my hand as the cab pulled up in front of us.

"You do that just by existing," he assured me, and I felt that warmth kindling in my stomach once more. How did he always know exactly the thing I needed to hear?

"Come on," I grimaced. "I suppose we've got to go back and face Priya."

"Don't worry about that yet," Rajesh opened the car door for me and ushered me inside. "We've still got a while before we have to see her again."

"And in the meantime?" I asked him.

"In the meantime," he suggested, "I say we make the most of the time we have together."

"And what do you mean by that?" I asked, and his eyes flashed suggestively at me.

"I've got a few ideas," he replied, and leaned across the cab to plant a soft, sweet kiss on my lips, and I suddenly knew without a doubt exactly what he had in mind for the two of us.

"I just want you to know, before we go any further," Priya looked at us over the top of the reading glasses she was wearing, "that I am severely unimpressed with the way the two of you have conducted yourselves over the last few weeks. *Severely.*"

I nodded, and looked down at my hands clasped in my lap. I felt as though I was being scolded by a school teacher. I had always been such a relentless goody-two-shoes that it felt profoundly wrong to be the subject of anyone's ire. Rajesh, ever the class bad boy, was reclining in his seat next to me taking the telling-off like he was used to them.

"I understand," I replied, my voice small and nervous. I didn't want to give her any reason to pounce on me, but I needed her to know that this wasn't how I was going to act every time she landed me on a new assignment.

"And you, Rajesh?" She turned her attention to him, looking at him expectantly. He lifted his gaze to meet hers and raised his eyebrows.

"Didn't you hire me because of my 'anarchic spirit'?" He asked, making air-quotes as though he was directly pulling words from her mouth. She tightened her lips, but didn't argue.

"I think it's worth restating that if you ever go after a story like this without my knowledge or consent again, you'll both be fired," she went on. "No questions. No second chances. Is that clear?"

We both nodded, even Rajesh managing to keep his mouth shut for the time being, even though I could tell he was itching to jump in with some other smart comment. He must have realized that our jobs weren't safe quite yet.

"But this..." Priya gestured to the article we'd written together back in the hotel room. "This is good. This is great."

I let out a long sigh of relief. It washed through my body, and I had to fight the urge to punch the air. I figured it wouldn't be the most professional course of action, and I didn't want to push my luck, given what we had just done to Priya and The Chronicle.

"I'm willing to give you both a pass, this time." She looked at us both threateningly, over the top of her glasses. "Let's not pretend you didn't betray my trust with this. And I understand that you were chasing down a big story, but you know I'll support you whenever and wherever I can with these kinds of projects. I just need you to be honest with me."

"We will," I blurted out, and noticed that Rajesh was staying pointedly quiet. I guessed he didn't want to agree to anything that he wasn't sure he could stick to. I shot him a look that told him to agree, for my sake as much as his.

"We will," he echoed, nudging his knee up against mine underneath the table in an attempt to comfort me. His touch helped, even though I knew we weren't free and clear quite yet.

"And now, the other issue," she sighed, pulling off her glasses and pinching the bridge of her nose between her fingers. "Someone – and I don't want to take names, but someone – reached out to me to let me know that the two of you had started a relationship. Is that true?"

I took a deep breath. There was no point in lying to her any longer. The truth was already out there, and the last thing I wanted was to have to hide this relationship any longer, not when it had made me so happy. Rajesh reached over and wound his fingers around mine, then looked back at Priya.

"Yes, it's true," he admitted. "We're together."

She looked at us, and a flicker of exhaustion passed across her face. It was clear that everything that had happened over the last few days had taken its toll on her as much as it had on us. She looked between us, and shook her head. She couldn't even muster much anger, even though I could tell she wanted to.

"I just want you to know that this is completely against company policy and with everything else you guys have already done, I would be completely within my rights to fire you both with no notice," she pointed out sharply. I nodded, my heart beating fast in my chest, and I exchanged a look with Rajesh. He didn't take his eyes from Priya and squeezed my hand comfortingly.

"But considering the article you guys just handed in," she reasoned. "And considering the kind of interest this is going to pull in for us, I'm willing to make an exception. Just for now."

I let out a long breath. I looked over at Rajesh, who beamed at me widely.

"But you have to keep your relationship firmly out of the office," she warned us. "I don't want to hear anyone else talking about this, I don't want you two to so much as exchange a flirty look as long as you're within these walls, is that clear?"

"That's totally clear," I nodded, the words falling out of me in relief. My shoulders sagged and I wanted to get to my feet and dance around the room, to plant a kiss on Rajesh's lips and hell, maybe Priya's too, just to thank her. But I kept my celebration to a small clenched fist by my side, the mildest acknowledgement that this had gone our way. I couldn't believe, after everything that had happened, that we had actually pulled this off. It had actually gone our way.

"Now, I need to get to editing this for release tomorrow," she nodded towards the story. "I'll let you guys have one last look at it before it goes to press. In the meantime, go home and get some rest, and I'll expect you back in tomorrow morning. Is that alright?"

"That's perfect," Rajesh got to his feet. "Thank you, Priya. Thanks for having faith in the two of us."

"You better not give me a reason to doubt it again," she warned him, and he offered her one of his dazzling smiles. She couldn't help but return it.

"Out of my sight, the two of you!" She ordered playfully, and we turned and headed out of the room towards Rajesh's office. As soon as the door was closed behind us, I tossed my arms around his neck and he swept me off my feet and spun me around.

"I can't believe it," he laughed. "This is amazing!"

"It all turned out for the best, right?" I asked, pulling back and looking at him, and he kissed me, tightening his grip on my waist.

"I would never have been with you if it hadn't been for this trip," he remarked, his voice dropping to a murmur as he brushed his nose across mine. "I don't think this could have turned out any better."

"Only a few weeks ago you didn't want me coming with you," I reminded him playfully, and he kissed me again.

"Let me show you how much you've changed my mind," he murmured in my ear, in a tone that told me exactly where this was going.

"Rajesh!" I squealed as his hand travelled down my back to cup my backside. "We're in the office…"

My protests faded off as he kissed my neck, and I closed my eyes and tried to remember exactly why we shouldn't do this. Nothing else seemed to matter outside of his hands on my skin, his mouth brushing up my throat.

"Just this once," he breathed. "I've always wanted to fool around at the office. After this, nothing, I promise."

"Just to get it out of our systems?" I suggested, trying to come up with an excuse that would let me go through with this. Because I wanted this, badly – but I knew it could land us in serious trouble.

"Just to get it out of our systems," he agreed. "Though I'm not sure there's much I can do to convince me to keep my hands off you."

"Mmm…" I purred as he stroked his fingers up my thigh, pushing up my skirt. I glanced out, back towards the office – the glass was so frosted in the tiny window in the door that I was sure no one would see us. Or at least, I was willing to take that risk.

He hitched me up on to the desk, and I pulled him in close so we could kiss properly; our tongues intertwined, and the fire flared up in my stomach once more. The excitement of keeping my job matched with the knowledge that my by-line was going to appear on one of the biggest articles that The Chronicle had ever put out was a heady mix, and when I threw in the urgent little moans Rajesh was letting out against my ear as his fingers sank into my skin, I could hardly restrain myself.

He reached down and pulled down my underwear, letting them drop to the floor beneath us – and before I knew it, he had dipped into his pocket and pulled out a condom. He flashed me a playful smile as he pulled his trousers down and swiftly sheathed himself, and I bit my lip excitedly.

"You came prepared for this, didn't you?" I teased, and he raised his eyebrows.

"Can you blame me?" he replied, catching my leg and pushing it back so that he could press himself against my entrance. I bit my lip as he slowly eased himself inside of me, doing my best to keep the little excited noises emanating from me to a minimum. Just think of the trouble we'd be in if we got caught – as he pushed himself all the way inside me, that only served to excite me more. I gasped and clutched at his back as he penetrated me, lifting my leg up so he could get in deep. We hadn't done this a lot yet, but it was already so good that I couldn't wait to see how amazing it would be in a few weeks, months, years.

We moved fast, his head pressed into my shoulder, knowing that we didn't have a lot of time before someone would notice that the two of us had vanished off together. I grinned, and lightly sank my teeth into his still-clothed shoulder; he let out a groan, and turned to kiss me once more, slowing briefly as though savouring the moment again. I ran my fingers through his hair, pulling him close, and remembering the first time I'd seen him in this very office. How sure I had been even then that he was something special, that he would become something important to me. Little did I know just how deep it would go.

Speaking of deep, he thrust into me as hard as he could, drawing a little squeak out from between my lips, and I realized that I was close, closer than I had realized. I tipped my head back and he greedily ran his lips up my throat, tasting me, touching me, consuming me.

And then I came. The orgasm burst through me, the flames of it licking around the base of my feet and up each of my limbs in turn, my skin prickling and one shoe falling off my foot as my toes curled in pleasure. Moments later, he found his own release inside me, plunging deep and then holding himself still for a moment as his entire body shuddered. Once he had come back to his senses, he quickly glanced over his shoulder and then pulled out of me, rolling the condom off and disposing of it.

"That was amazing," I breathed, patting down my hair and going to grab my shoe as the two of us got redressed as fast as we could manage.

"Now, let's get out of here before anyone notices," Rajesh hurried me along, and I grinned at him.

"Hey, I think this was your idea, not mine," I reminded him, and he quickly pulled me in for a kiss. For a second, I forgot why we were in a hurry and kissed him back – the man I loved, the man who I wanted to be with more than anything. And then, he pulled back and I came back to my senses. He waited till I was decent and then opened the door, and the two of us stepped out into the world together once more.

Epilogue

"How are you doing?" Rajesh asked, flopping down on the couch next to me. I leaned over and he pulled me against his chest, the two of us assuming our natural posture, learned from weeks of routine. We'd spend all day at work doing our level best to ignore each other, and then as soon as we got back to his place, we would allow ourselves to act like the couple we were.

It had been a few months since we'd come back from the conference, and it had been nothing but go since then. The story had gone out a few days after we'd returned, and while it met with major backlash from the two companies which it concerned (unsurprisingly), it turned into something of a phenomenon for The Chronicle. We received a special commendation from a national journalism board for our work, and it was up for a couple of awards over the next few months. So, with my first article, I could well have become an award-winning journalist which wasn't a bad way to start. Since then, Priya had kept a close eye on me and stuck me to mostly doing smaller, local stories, and I was happy to build her trust in me from the ground up once more. I was still working there, and so was Rajesh, and that's what mattered. Even if I did sometimes get a little jealous about how interesting the stories that he got to cover were.

More importantly, though, the two of us had been thriving, even though we were forced to keep our relationship out of the office. No one else we worked with, except Priya, knew anything about the fact we were dating and I was perfectly happy keeping it that way. Sometimes, it would have been nice to boast about my amazing boyfriend to the people I worked with, but for the time being, my family would just have to get used to me bending their ears about how great he was.

They started off a little uncertain about our relationship, and I couldn't say I blamed them. After how heartbroken I'd been by Akshay, and knowing that this was a colleague of mine who was a little more experienced in the dating world than I was, I knew it was always going to take my mother some time to come around to him. But as soon as they met him, everything changed. They adored him, and as soon as he left after the first time they met each other, they couldn't stop going on about how charming and handsome and intelligent he was.

"I can't wait until he's part of the family," my mother remarked as she put away some plates, and I rolled my eyes.

"I don't know about that," I protested, and she glanced over at me with an incredulous expression on her face.

"Oh, he's going to ask soon," she promised me. "The way he looks at you, it's obvious."

"I know Rajesh, and I don't—"

"And I know men who are in love with their women," she cut me off firmly. "And that's what I see when I look at the two of you."

"Whatever you say, mama," I muttered to myself, knowing there was nothing I could do to dissuade her.

But soon, I started wondering if maybe she was right. Sometimes, I would catch Rajesh looking at me and it felt as though there was a glint in his eyes that spoke to something more, something deeper. The very look he had in his eyes at that moment, actually, now that I thought of it.

I turned my head to look up at him.

"What are you thinking?" I asked, and he shrugged, playing with a strand of my hair.

"Just how happy I am to be home with you," he remarked with a smile and I leaned up to kiss him.

"You're such an old charmer," I teased lightly, and he brushed his nose against mine.

"Not so old," he protested, and I grinned and snuggled back into his chest.

It hadn't been so long since I'd met his family. I could tell that, same as mine, they'd been a little suspicious. The way we'd gotten together had been a little odd; I had to give them that. But, nervous as I had been, Rajesh assured me that it went well and they had loved me almost as much as my family had loved him. I wondered if that had got him thinking more about marriage – it certainly had the question in my head more often. But, right then and there, I couldn't think about anything but how happy I was to be with him, and how I would be happy if I could stay in this moment forever.

It was strange, only a few months before, the two of us had both been broken by break-ups. After Akshay had left me, I had retreated into myself, sure that no man would ever be able to take me and everything I wanted for my life and love me despite it. But Rajesh had. He had seen me as I was, and he had accepted me without a second thought. He loved me fiercely, so fiercely sometimes that I wondered if anything would ever sway it. He didn't want me to change, wasn't expecting me to give anything up to be with him. He wanted me as I was, and that was more than I could ever hope for. It was more than I deserved, and I thanked god every day that he had chosen me to share his life with.

"What are you thinking?" Rajesh turned the question around on me, and I closed my eyes and nestled into his chest.

"Nothing important," I replied. "Just how happy I am to be here."

"Glad we can agree on something," he locked his fingers around my middle, and we lay there for a moment like that. And then, he spoke again.

"You know I love you, right?" he asked softly, his voice so quiet I almost couldn't hear it. I nodded.

"I love you too," I affirmed. "Always."

"Always," he replied, and he caught my chin and tilted it up towards him to kiss me. And I lost myself to the feel of his lips on mine, of his arms around me, and thanked everything good in the world that the universe had delivered this man to me.